SANTA'S FAVORITE

MADELEINE TAYLOR

Edited by Claire Jarrett

Cover design by Meg Sayers

1

Is he really staring at me again? I narrow my eyes at Santa, who's been ogling me each time I walk past. His big stage on the ground floor has been strategically placed at the far end of Bergman's, and he's sitting in an elaborately decorated sleigh filled with presents, led by a group of animatronic reindeer. The Norwegian pines that surround the stage look like a real forest, and the long winter wonderland walkway that leads up to him is simply irresistible to kids; moving trees, fake snow and Santa's deep voice welcoming everyone with a 'Merry Christmas' draws them in like bees to honey.

While parents are perusing the aisles of this exclusive department store in Manhattan, kids wait in line for their turn on his lap, to hand him their letters and to have their picture taken with him.

His beard has come loose on one side and his gold half-glasses are sitting crooked on his nose. I can feel his eyes on my behind and let out a groan of frustration as I realize I've forgotten the item I came to pick up in the first place. *Fuck. Now I have to walk past him again.*

My mind is all over the place today; it's the third time I've been lost in my own thoughts, forgetting stuff on the wish list that keeps growing on my tablet. Unfortunately, my personal to-do list keeps growing too, and as I'm working overtime at Bergman's over my Christmas break, I'm lagging behind on my studies. *Just six more days*, I tell myself. Then it will be full steam ahead and I'll be able to focus on my exams and apply for my legal internships.

The store's VIP customers have an easy life when it comes to their Christmas shopping. All they have to do is send through their shopping list and underpaid suckers like me make sure their gifts are wrapped up beautifully and sent to their family members, kids, wives, husbands or lovers along with a handwritten card so no one would ever entertain the idea that they haven't put the effort in themselves. We even have phone consultations with the big spenders and give them suggestions on additions or upgrades.

I turn back and head for the jewelry counter to pick up the gold watch with inscription. Bergman's spans six floors and over a million square feet, so wasting fifteen minutes before arriving upstairs empty handed is not an option, especially over the busy holidays. As much as this job bores me, I need it too, and I don't intend to get fired just before Christmas.

"All done." My colleague who mans the jewelry counter hands me the watch and I turn it around to check the inscription that says, '*For Renate, with love, Henry*'. Henry didn't even pick it himself; I did that. He told me he wanted to buy his girlfriend a watch and that he believed she preferred gold to silver, although he wasn't entirely sure. When I asked him what inscription he would like, he asked me for suggestions. Ninety percent of my clients are men.

They love the easy way out, and more often than not, they ask me to pick something for the ladies in their lives.

"Everything is in the box," my colleague continues. "Warranty, extra strap in camel leather, receipt for you to email. Do you have any more inscriptions for me today?"

"So far, no. But the last minute orders keep coming in so I might be back." I give him a smile and a wave and brace myself for another walk past creepy Santa. I could make a detour, but since I'm wearing a Bergman's name tag, shoppers assume I'm part of the floor team and stop me every few steps for enquiries, so I'd rather take the quickest route to the staff elevators.

The ground floor always annoys me as it's where most of the festivities happen. 'Santaland'—an area that provides the whole Christmas experience for adults and kids alike—currently covers three quarters of the ground floor. There's the winter wonderland walk with Santa's stage, the interactive nativity exhibition with real animals and actors playing Mary and Joseph, and there's the huge fake Christmas tree in the atrium that reaches all the way up to the third floor. The VM team have sprayed it with something pine scented that's so synthetic it's making me nauseous. Each booth representing a brand, or a range of products, has its own little twist on Christmas and with all of them competing under one roof, it's culminating into an insane mix of decorations, lights, glitter, sounds and smells that clash like thunder. Our customers love it though, and Bergman's has been awarded *Best Visual Merchandiser* three years in a row.

I'm not a big fan of Christmas and working here right now is giving me Christmas overload. The carols that are constantly on repeat, the artificial smells that are way too strong to be pleasant, and the annoyingly chirpy 'Merry Christmas' messages and enquiries from colleagues each time I pass them. 'What are you doing over Christmas?', 'How's your tree looking?', 'Big family gathering?'

The excitement they display is beyond me. My family consists of my mother and me, and neither of us cares. We don't have the best Christmas memories and my mom was never able to afford decorations or presents when I was younger. She even used to take me to work with her at the diner on Christmas Eve, as she was unable to find a babysitter over the holidays. I didn't mind back then as I was quite happy keeping myself busy with a coloring book and a hot chocolate, but it did sting sometimes when friends from school told me about how their parents had spoilt them with lavish gifts when we were back at school. Now, looking around and seeing what Christmas has become, I despise it even more. It's a commercial circus and everyone falls for it like a fool.

Quickening my pace, I keep my eyes fixed on the elevators ahead of me as I pass Santa again. Thankfully, he's got a toddler on each knee and is too busy to notice me this time. I hear both the children and the parents surrounding him burst out in laughter and find it hard to imagine that he's actually funny. Perhaps he's not that bad at his job, but I'd still rather see him go. I've worked here three years now and the Santa we had before was a lovely old man, but I guess he's retired now.

"Lucy, wait!" I smile when my colleague and friend Bridget quickly slips into the elevator with me before the doors close. "Don't you just love Christmas?" she asks, holding up a huge cinnamon cookie wedged between a napkin. "Free cookies and lots of happy people." Pressing the button for the sixth floor where the staff break room, the mail room and our gift-wrapping room are situated, she takes a bite and holds it out for me. When I decline, she laughs and shakes her head. "Never mind. I know how you feel about Christmas."

"Sorry. Just not hungry," I say, not wanting to come across as a miserable Christmas grinch. Bridget never complains about her job. She's one of those super optimistic people with a wonderful work ethic and sometimes I wish I could be more like her. We're polar opposites, but we got along from the first day I started here, and she makes me laugh when I'm going through stressful times. In the looks department, we couldn't be more different either. I'm dressed in a pencil skirt, a white blouse and high heels that make up for my height. My black shoulder-length hair is immaculately styled and my ever-present red lipstick reapplied hourly. Bridget is dressed in black slacks, the same white blouse Bergman's provides, and comfortable black flats. Her dark curls are sitting on top of her head in a messy jumble and she rarely shows off her shapely hourglass figure I'm so envious of. Even though eating outside the break room is against the store's policy, she somehow manages to snack all day long without anyone noticing, and she's constantly on her phone too.

The elevator ride always seems to take forever but there's something soothing about the silence in here. The ground floor is for jewelry, cosmetics, and Santaland, the first floor is womenswear, the second menswear, the third childrenswear and toys, the fourth interior, the fifth electronics and besides the various staff areas the sixth floor also houses an assortment of restaurants and a small 'adult' section.

"Anything saucy?" I ask when I see her grin while scrolling through her messages.

"Yeah. This guy Jack sent me an interesting picture. Wanna see?"

I laugh and raise a brow at her. "Gross no. Unless Jack is short for Jackie, I'm good." Bridget's divorce got finalized six months ago, and she's been hooked on dating apps ever since. "Are you going to meet up with him?"

"Maybe. There's someone else I like more, but I'm leaving him hanging in case I get a better offer. It's almost Christmas, so it's not like we'll be meeting up until January." She changes the subject as the elevator stops on the third floor and another staff member steps inside. "Anyway, I know it's temporary as you just want to earn some extra cash, but how are you finding your first full-time week?"

"It's actually harder than I thought," I say. "Tiring more than anything. I don't know how you do this day in, day out. And especially right now... Fake enthusiasm, the carols and so much sparkle that my eyes hurt." I rub them demonstratively. "And then there's Santa downstairs. He's been undressing me with his eyes each time I walk past and I'm thinking of taking it to HR. He even winked at me the other day. That's not okay, right?"

"Santa?" Bridget stares at me, open-mouthed.

"Yeah." I return her stare. "Why are you looking at me like that?"

She laughs as we step out onto the sixth floor. "Santa's not a man. Santa Claudia as I'm calling her this year is actually a woman." Reaching the black door that says, 'staff only', she swipes her pass and lets us into the small gift-wrapping room that we share with the team of personal shoppers, then switches on the kettle.

"What?" I put the watch aside because wrapping it can wait until we've finished this intriguing conversation. Taking a striped candy cane out of the large bowl next to the kettle, I start picking at the wrapper while perching on the edge of the table. "You're messing with me, right?"

"No, I'm not; I saw her in the dressing room this morning." Bridget adds tea bags to two mugs and taps her fingers impatiently while she waits for the water to boil. "If you came in early and got changed here like you're supposed to do instead of crossing town in your uniform, you would have seen her too. You know what? Come to think of it, she did look a little..."

"A little what?"

"A little gay?" Bridget chuckles and winks at me while she pours the water and hands me a mug. "It was her energy, I suppose. Not sure how to explain it, but I felt this vibe coming off her." She quietly studies me to gauge my reaction. "So, the fact that she's checking you out might not be a bad thing."

"Even if she's a woman, that doesn't mean she can behave like that," I say, pretending to be unaffected by this new information. Truth is though, whether it be wrong or right, knowing Santa is a woman changes everything. It's not very often that women flirt with me as they just assume that I'm straight, and I suddenly feel oddly flattered.

"No, I suppose not." Bridget dips the rest of her cookie in her tea and leans over the table. "Well, if you want my advice, just tell her that you're not interested. If she doesn't stop, then take it to HR."

2

———

Hearing a whistle behind me as I cross the ground floor, I turn around. My mouth falls open when I realize it's Santa, who's tidying her 'workspace' after her shift.

Santa pulls down her beard to give me a crooked smile while she bends down to pick up a piece of red wrapping paper. The department store gives out small presents and candy to the kids and despite the cleaning team of elves who sweep the floors three times a day, there's still wrapping paper and pieces of ribbon everywhere. Now that Bergman's is closed and the kids are gone, Santa's less subtle with her flirtations and she stares me up and down like I'm dinner.

I walk up to her, pretending to be offended, but I can't help but smile back when our eyes meet. Hers are very, very blue. "Are you flirting with me, Santa?"

"Maybe." Santa's eyes pull into narrow slits and although her beard has snapped back into place, I know there's an amused expression behind it. "Are you trying to get my attention..." Her big, fake belly bounces as she jumps off the stage and her eyes lower to the name badge on my chest. "Lucy?"

I let out an exasperated gasp and stare at her. "I'm most certainly not."

"Then why did you just walk past me three times? In that sexy pencil skirt."

"It's my work uniform." I roll my eyes. "I'm sure you've noticed all the women here wear it."

Santa inches closer and lowers her voice. "Not true. Most of the women wear slacks." She lowers her gaze, resting her eyes on my cleavage. "And even if they do wear a skirt, they certainly don't wear it like you. Not with killer heels and a white blouse that's buttoned down just enough to show the edge of a black lace bra." She points to my legs. "And not with sheer pantyhose. Or are they thigh high stockings? I have a thing for stockings."

My slight annoyance is replaced by a blush, and I hope the lights from the Christmas tree next to her stage work in my favor. I should be offended by her objectifying me like this but instead, it sends a twitch between my legs. The fact that she's standing so close doesn't help either; I can feel her breath on my face and her voice sounds deliciously intimate.

Maybe this whole Christmas spectacle isn't going to be so bad after all if I have some entertainment in the form of flirtation to look forward to. I've seen her smile now; it's dazzling, and her piercing eyes have captured my curiosity. Ignoring her last question, I shake my head and do my best to paint on a more serious expression. "Do you flirt with all the women who walk past you?"

Santa looks around to make sure no one is listening, and then turns back to me, her eyes burning into mine. "Only with the ones I'd like to fuck."

"What?" My eyebrows shoot up and I bring a hand to my mouth. I'm a little outraged, my body is doing its own thing and I feel hot and flustered. Being a law student, conflict brews inside me. This is so wrong, yet I seem to like what's happening here. Subconsciously I rake a hand through my dark hair and wonder if my eyeliner is still in place.

Santa simply shrugs. "You heard me." Her confidence is through the roof, and I can't help but laugh because she's just too much.

"How come no one has reported you to HR yet?"

"You're the only one I've flirted with so far."

Her flattery is working and although I'm pretty sure she's lying, I still like her answer. "How do you know I won't report you?"

"I'm hoping you won't." Santa pauses. "I'm hoping you'll just tell me to back off if I'm overstepping. Tell me, and I'll leave you alone. Do you want me to stop?"

I decide not to answer her question as I'm not ready to admit how much I'm loving the attention. "How do you even know I'm into women?"

"Trust me, I know. I've seen you looking at me."

"Have you now?" My voice is dripping with sarcasm but truthfully, she's right. Ever since Bridget told me she was a woman I've been on the ground floor an awful lot. Remembering I'm supposed to finish my order, and that there are another six lists for me to complete before midnight, I hold up the box I'm carrying. "Well, I'm just here because I forgot to bring this; It needs adding to a jewelry order. I'm sorry to disappoint you but I wasn't walking past to get your attention."

"Hmm..." Santa nods slowly as she finger-combs her long white beard, never taking her eyes off me. "Do you work in the jewelry department?"

"No. I'm a personal shopper. Just getting the Christmas madness out of the way before we close next week." I study her with an amused smile, not quite ready to leave just yet. Her straightforwardness is setting me on fire, and I don't even know what she looks like. "But my guess is you'll be working over Christmas."

"True. I am Santa after all. I'll be here until next week, and then I'll be spreading the Christmas joy in private New York households." She points to my package. "With bags full of the goodies you're preparing."

"Is that how it works? I didn't know."

"Yeah. Wealthy people pay good money to escape the Christmas stress. They put in their order, you collect the presents, wrap them up beautifully and personalize them, then someone prepares the Santa bags, and if they pay the extra thousand dollars, Santa personally drops them off on Christmas Eve and Christmas Day." She pats her chest. "With Santa being me and a dozen other Bergman's Santas."

I tilt my head and study her. "Forgive me for saying this, but I'm actually surprised Bergman's gave you the gig; you're not the most convincing Santa I've ever seen."

Now it's Santa's turn to gasp, and she pulls down her beard again, giving me sight of luscious lips and a neat row of very white teeth. "Are you saying I suck at being Santa?"

I laugh and shake my head in amusement. "Come on; you have to admit that your beard and your glasses aren't the best props and despite the subtle face paint, you still look too young. I just think that they could have easily found someone a little more convincing. Plus, you're a woman." Holding up a hand, I add: "Truthfully, I didn't register the fact that you're a woman at first, but surely the kids must notice when they sit on your lap and hear your voice."

"You mean this voice?" she says, putting on a low and raspy voice that sends a chill down my spine. She climbs back on stage and sits down on her sleigh, her arms resting on the ornate, red velvet covered armrests. When she widens her legs, hunches her back and leans forward, her whole demeanor changes and I must admit that she's actually very good. "It may be my first time as Santa and I might have to get some better glue for my beard as toddlers keep pulling at it, but believe me; the kids love me and they totally fall for it," she continues in her Santa voice, drawing the words out slowly like an old man would.

I'm silent for a beat, admittedly impressed by her performance. "Okay, you sound pretty convincing."

"Thank you." Santa's gaze drops to my legs again, no doubt still wondering about my stockings, before she turns her attention to the package I now have clutched against my chest. "So, what have you got in that little box, Lucy? Want to come sit on Santa's lap and share?"

My manager calls my name from the bauble section, and I straighten myself and clear my throat, letting Santa know our conversation is over. *Fuck.* Her request has aroused me and now all I can think of is sitting on her lap.

"No, I have work to do." Curious to find out what she looks like without her Santa disguise, I'm contemplating going up to the dressing room for a while, assuming she'll be there to get changed, but I really don't have time. "What's your name?"

"Zelda."

"Oh." I kind of expected her to stay in her Santa role and I'm pleasantly surprised that she didn't. "I like it." Giving my manager a wave to let her know I'm coming, I add: "It was interesting to meet you, Zelda. I'll see you around."

3

It's two a.m. by the time I'm in bed. Even naked on top of the covers, I'm warm and I wonder if I turned the heating up too high. After a quick shower and a pack of instant noodles, I still feel shaky and I realize it's not from hunger or tiredness.

Santa—or Zelda—has my mind spinning with fantasies and I know I won't be able to sleep unless I can find a way to relax. Replaying our conversation and remembering her smile, an intense flash of arousal shoots to my pussy, making my body ache with need.

'*Only with women I want to fuck.*' Jesus, could she have been any more direct? It's been a while since I was so sexually drawn to someone. Sure, I've had the occasional fling here and there, but I don't remember the last time I craved someone that specifically or fantasized about sex. I've only talked to her once but clearly that was enough for her to capture my undivided attention. God, I'm a sucker. One day I'm considering reporting her and the next, I'm having erotic daydreams about her.

Confused and conflicted, I let out a deep sigh as I glance at the pile of draft application letters for legal internships on the desk opposite the bed. I need to make sure they're absolutely perfect before I post them in January, and I planned on editing at least one of them tonight but I'm too tired to move. I asked for overtime in my winter break so I'd have a small financial buffer for next year, when I'll be doing internships and may have to cut down my hours at Bergman's. Once I graduate and have my J.D, I'll hopefully find a job as a paralegal while I focus on my bar exam, and then I can finally quit working as a personal shopper.

Studying is time-consuming and women have been the last thing on my mind for the past three years. Bridget keeps telling me that I should be dating at twenty-seven, but I just don't know where to find the time and anyway, I'm never interested in taking it beyond the first night.

Unlike most people in my class, I don't come from a wealthy family, and although I have a scholarship, I still have to work on the side to pay for the rent on my dorm room and to cover my living costs. Lucky for me, my lovely but noisy roommate Shelley is with her parents over the Christmas break, and the silence is blissful without her laughing out loud while she watches Netflix in bed and crunches her way through at least three packets of potato chips a night.

Between studying and my part-time job, there's little time left for fun and I'm okay with that. Shelley and Bridget keep me entertained when I need it, and with only one year left before I graduate, I don't want to waste money I don't have. I'll start having fun once I receive my first proper paycheck and I'm already dreaming about splashing out on some expensive lingerie before meeting co-workers for cocktails downtown. I've worked hard to get to where I am and I usually won't allow myself to get distracted, but Zelda is distracting beyond belief and I'm loving it.

I can't even say it's a physical thing as I've only seen her in her Santa disguise. No, the attraction is different with her. It's her energy and her confidence that is drawing me in. Her boldness and playfulness have me curious, and there's so much I want to know. Why is she working as Santa? What's her background? Her name is interesting, and I can't imagine traditional parents naming their child Zelda. But most importantly—what does she look like? All I know is that she has an amazing smile, intense blue eyes, and that she's into women, of course. Somehow, she knew I was, too.

Most people assume I'm straight, as I look very feminine. My hair is always immaculately styled and my signature feline black eyeliner and red lipstick never out of place. I've been told many times my near-black eyes are my selling point, which is why I accentuate them. With a beautiful Venezuelan mother and from what I've heard, a very average looking American father, I'm lucky to have my mother's exotic looks.

Even when I'm not at Bergman's, I tend to wear the same type of clothes I wear at work; pencil skirts, white blouses and black heels. Keeping it simple and timeless is key as I don't have the budget to stay on top of fashion, but I need to look presentable in class. I guess you could say I look fairly conservative, although some—like Zelda—may argue that it's rather sexy. My thigh high stockings—Zelda was right about them—are my only small form of rebellion. What I wear under my clothes is a treat to myself, my little secret, which is why I never get dressed at work. The black, lace bodice that I wore today is extremely low-cut at the front and with the matching garter belt, my lingerie is not meant for my colleagues to see.

A shiver runs through me as I imagine Zelda pulling me onto her lap and finding what's underneath my skirt as she hikes it up with her white-gloved hands. Is she into lingerie? I'd be surprised if she wasn't. With another week to go before Bergman's closes for Christmas, it's likely that we'll see each other a lot in passing, and I might even get the opportunity to talk to her again. I might even get the chance to sit on her lap... That last thought drives me crazy and unable to stand the throbbing in my pussy any longer, I blindly reach for the vibrator on my nightstand, turn it on to the highest setting, and slide it between my legs. With Shelley gone, I've been using it every night, grateful for the privacy I'm so rarely blessed with. A groan escapes me as the device hits my clit, and I slowly roll my hips as I get used to the intense vibrations that will soon soothe my aching need. As I slide it up and down between my folds, covering my pussy in my own juices, my thoughts are with Zelda. I think of kissing her and it only takes me seconds to balance on the edge of an orgasm. *Fuck. Why am I so into her?* Removing the vibrator, I lie very still, my breathing quick and heavy as I stare up at the ceiling. Withholding is hard, but I know it will make my orgasm way more intense if I do.

After a minute or so, I slowly bring the vibrator back down and try to concentrate on the memory of Zelda's lips that flashed a smile at me when she pulled down her beard. God, what I wouldn't give to have those lips between my legs right now. This toy is great, but nothing compares to the real thing. I moan as my climax builds, and I lift my hips with a quick intake of breath. Shaking wildly, I let the warm waves of ecstasy wash over me while I murmur a curse. As expected, it's intense and the throbbing in my clit almost hurts before it slowly starts to subside, bringing me back to reality. I breathe in deeply and run a hand over my swollen pussy, drawing out the last aftershocks until I finally fall asleep.

4

_____

"What's up with you?" Bridget asks as we're preparing the gift-wrapping area for our shift. "You seem a little absent this morning." She checks her orders and reads through the special requests, making sure she has the right materials to give her customers exactly what they want. A selection of luxurious wrapping papers is hanging on the wall behind the long table that holds drawers with various rolls of ribbons, cards, scissors and any kind of stationary we could possibly need. "Are you okay?"

"It's nothing," I mumble, scrolling through my tablet. I feel a stab of disappointment that I have very few items to pick up on the ground floor. Zelda took over my dreams last night and even though I know it's silly, I'm unable to think of anything else but her. "Just not too excited about my orders today."

"Why is that?" Bridget takes my tablet, scans my orders and turns to me with a puzzled expression. "These are easy, Lucy. You won't even have to wrap anything complicated; it's all very straightforward. Plus, unlike me, you won't have to deal with Versace Paul. He always gets on my nerves." She pauses and arches a brow at me. "Unless you were hoping to see more of Santa Claudia?" The last question is drawn out in a teasing tone, and I can't help but laugh.

"Shut up." I give Bridget a playful slap on her behind, and her eyes widen as she turns to me.

"Oh my God, you really are into her!"

Averting my gaze, I sigh and hope Bridget won't see the color on my cheeks. "Maybe a little. She flirted with me yesterday and it's just…" I pause, not sure how to explain my sudden interest in Santa. "It's just nice to feel desired again."

"So, let me get this straight. She flirted with you again and now that you know Santa's a woman, you're suddenly okay with it?"

"Flirting is an understatement; she was coming on strong." I shrug. "And yes, I guess it's a little fucked up, but I don't mind her coming onto me anymore. In fact, I like it."

"You're right; that is messed up, you dirty girl," Bridget teases. "But it does mean I was right; she *is* gay. Did you guys talk in the dressing room or something?" She chuckles and pokes my arm. "Or did you do something other than talking in the dressing room?"

"We didn't do anything," I exclaim, holding up both hands. "We just talked after she'd finished her shift. I don't even know what she looks like, but she seems…"

"She seems what?"

I shake my head and groan in frustration because I know Bridget won't let this go until I voice my thoughts. "I don't know. She seems kind of sexy."

"Sexy?" Bridget shakes her head with a smile. "Lucy's got a thing for Santa. This is so funny; I can't wait to tell the girls over lunch."

"Don't you dare." I shoot her a warning glare.

"Just kidding, honey." Bridget hands me her tablet and

takes mine. "Here, I'll trade you. I have shitty orders anyway and I hate waiting for the elevator so please go ahead and enjoy my ground floor visits. If you don't tell, I won't."

"Really?"

"Hell, yeah. You'll be here longer than me but if that's what you want, by all means knock yourself out."

"There's my Lucy." The sound of my name makes me jump as I come out of the cubical in the staff restrooms. Zelda is by the washbasins, rinsing her hands. "You look ravishingly beautiful as always."

"Thank you. I'd say the same for you," I retort in a joking tone. "But you know..." I wiggle a finger at her outfit, and she laughs.

"Probably not the best look for seducing someone," she agrees, drying her hands before adjusting her jacket. "But one can try, right?"

"True. No harm in trying." I shoot her a sideways glance and note that she's staring at me. "How's your day?" Hoping Zelda won't notice how thrown I am by her flattery or simply being in the same room with her, I focus on washing my hands as looking at her makes me forget who I am.

"It's great." Zelda pulls down her beard and shoots me a sexy smile. "Fun, actually. I didn't think I'd enjoy being Santa as much; it's not something I normally do, but I'm having a great time with it. The kids have been good so far. Well, most of them, anyway."

"What is it that you normally do?" I ask, even more curious now.

"Oh, you know, this and that." Zelda lifts her wig and hat, so her face is exposed before pulling a contour pencil from one of her long pockets. She starts topping up her face paint and it looks like she knows what she's doing. "The toddlers keep smudging it," she says, accentuating the wrinkle lines between her bushy stick-on eyebrows. They're prominent, but from what I can see, she's very, very attractive. "So, how's your day? I've enjoyed seeing you this morning."

Noting she hasn't answered my question, I decide not to pry any further. "You mean you've enjoyed staring at my ass?" I ask instead, knowing that's exactly what she's been doing. I've been having fun with Bridget's order list, walking past her at least twice an hour. Unlike last week, I've loved every second of her eyes roaming over me and I even looked back a couple of times to let her know the interest was mutual. The kids love her; I observed her from the perfume counter and couldn't help but laugh at her child-like enthusiasm as she interacted with them. Authentic or not, she does make a decent Santa after all.

"Come on, Lucy. You can't blame me when you're wearing a tight pencil skirt and sway your hips the way you do." She arches a brow as she looks down at my ass. "You're Santa's favorite."

"Santa's favorite, huh?"

"Yeah. I have a feeling you've been a good girl. And if that's true, Santa will take care of you." Zelda winks in a salacious manner that sends a flutter through my core. There's a loaded silence and it feels like the walls are closing in on us. I'm all too aware of my trembling limbs as she closes the distance between us while she continues. "But if you haven't been good..." She pauses. "If you've been bad, Lucy, then Santa will gladly take care of that too."

Her words cause my pulse to race and I have no idea how to reply to that, so I focus on rinsing the soap from my hands instead. Normally I would scold someone for talking to me like that, but it's like she's infiltrated my mind. The thing is, I don't really want her to stop because she seems to know exactly how to push my buttons. When I bend over the basin to reach for a paper towel, she comes up behind me and places her hands on my hips. The light touch alone makes me squirm and I can see the desire flaring up in my eyes as I watch us in the mirror. She's got me right where she wants me.

"Just tell me if you want me to stop," Zelda whispers in my ear when I straighten myself. "So, what's it going to be? Have you been good?" Her false beard tickles me as she traces her lips over my neck, then down to my shoulder and it's so thrilling that a moan escapes my mouth. "Or bad?" Suddenly, her hand lands hard on my behind and she follows this with a firm squeeze.

Startled, I gasp and turn around, and come face to face with her. I can still feel a sting where her hand landed and even though it's totally inappropriate, it's making me throb with a weird longing for more. Again, I say nothing because why on earth would I play along and answer a question like that? I'm grateful for her big Santa belly that's pushing me back against the basin as it's the only thing keeping some distance between us. Zelda excites me, thrills me and arouses me all at once, and right now, I have no idea what I would do if she came any closer. This is ridiculous; I'm not one for making out with a stranger in a restroom, I remind myself, and step to the side, needing space.

"No need to answer now, you have the afternoon to think about it," Zelda says in a low voice.

"How so?" I ask, not sure if I'm ready for what's coming.

"I noticed you were in early this morning, so I assume you're not working the late shift. Are you busy tonight?"

Her question startles me and my libido fires up as I contemplate my answer. This is getting real. "Not really. Why do you ask?" Cursing myself for the tremble in my voice, I fiddle with the paper towel and try to compose myself. I hope she won't see my shaking hands but I'm sure it's pretty obvious that she's got me very, very turned on.

"I'm asking because, as I confessed yesterday, I'd like to fuck you." Zelda crosses her arms in front of her chest, chuckling at my startled expression. "If you want that too, of course."

I study her to gauge if she's serious, then shake my head and laugh it off. "I heard you loud and clear the first time but it's a bit soon for that, don't you think? We don't even know each other." She locks her gaze with mine and the eye contact is electric. If I'm completely honest with myself, I wouldn't mind giving into her request as my body is begging me to do so, but it seems a little extreme. "I mean, I thought you were going to ask me out for dinner or something."

"I'll take you out for dinner." Zelda smirks and when I don't protest, she steps in front of me again. "After I've fucked you," she whispers, moving her thigh between my legs. "I'm sure we'll be very hungry afterward." Standing still for long moments, she brings her mouth close to mine and presses herself into me. I'm convinced she's going to kiss me and decide there and then that I wouldn't mind if she does. "Think about it."

Turning into a puddle, I let out the breath I've been holding and steady myself against the basin, gripping the edge of the cool surface. I'm dripping wet and the twitch between my legs is getting more intense by the second. Frankly, if she pushed into me a little harder, I think she could make me come. How does she do this to me? Women have turned me on before, but it was never like this, not so all-consuming, and all I can think of now is having her mouth on mine. She doesn't kiss me but tilts her head and lingers in a torturous teasing manner before she adjusts her beard, turns on her heel and heads for the door.

Fuck, I should have kissed her when I had the chance.

"Think about it," she repeats. "I live in Hell's Kitchen on 10th Avenue. There's a blue door next to a Chinese restaurant called Mei-Ling. I live on the third floor, be there at eight." Zelda looks over her shoulder. "Or don't. That's up to you, of course, but I can promise if you do come, you won't regret it."

5

Five hours later and I'm still shaking on my feet. The mix of unforgiving nerves and butterflies that settled deep in my core after Zelda left the bathroom have not subsided one bit. The way she pushed herself up against me while she stared at me with those incredible piercing blue eyes have left an intense craving in my body, and flashbacks have been haunting me for hours.

To distract myself, I've rushed up and down and back and forth, covering most of the store's floorspace while completing Bridget's orders in record time. She looks perplexed as I put down her pad, kick off my heels and make myself a coffee before I wrap my last present for the day. "Want one?"

"God no, it's way too late for coffee." Bridget shoots me a suspicious look. Don't tell me you're done already..." She wipes the last bits of ribbon from her side of the gift-wrapping table, then tilts her head as she studies me. "Girl, you look red-hot, have you been running a marathon?"

"I feel that way," I say, checking the time on my phone. There are two other personal shoppers here today but they're on the late shift, so we have the room to ourselves. "Almost done with forty-five minutes to spare."

"Good lord. Don't tell management or they'll replace me," Bridget jokes. "Are you studying tonight?"

Shaking my head, a small smile plays around my mouth while I take a sip of my coffee. "No, not tonight," I say, tearing a piece of shiny black wrapping paper from one of the big rolls. I carefully wrap the box that contains an exclusive bottle of perfume, then fold a gold ribbon around the neat package. I use a gold-inked Sharpie to write the matching black Christmas card that will be delivered with the present.

'*Happy Christmas to my sexy bunny. Hope to meet up again soon. Mr. F.*'

I think it's safe to assume this present will be going to someone's mistress.

"Then what are you doing?" Bridget nudges my arm. "Come on, Lucy. You look like you're up to no good and you know you can't keep secrets from me."

I hesitate for a beat, then say, "Zelda invited me over to her house."

Bridget looks puzzled. "Who's Zelda?"

"Santa. From downstairs," I clarify. "Her name is Zelda."

"Seriously? You have a date?" Bridget lifts herself onto the table and starts firing off questions. "Did she invite you for dinner? Is she cooking for you?"

I buy some time by pretending to look for the right address label for the present as I drop it into a shiny white paper Berman's gift bag. Should I tell her? How will it make me look? Being a law student, my reputation is everything to me, but Bridget knows me well and she's way more open-minded than my fellow students and lecturers. "No. She invited me for sex," I finally say, deciding to just confess.

"She totally came on to me in the restrooms earlier today; I actually thought she was going to kiss me for a moment."

"What?"

"Yeah, it was seriously hot."

"But you're not going, right?" Bridget narrows her eyes at me. "Are you actually going? It's a little soon, don't you think?"

"That's what I thought. It's certainly not an invitation I would normally accept. The last couple of times I've slept with a woman was during a night out and those are few and far apart. It was spontaneous, not planned; it's just easier when there's a bar and a bit of alcohol involved so you can forget about it the next day." I shrug. "But I suppose Zelda won't be at Bergman's for that long; it's almost Christmas so it's not like I'm going to see her after her Santa gig," I add, thinking out loud. "So, I might go; I haven't decided yet. Truth is, part of me wants to because I could really do with a good lay. It's been a while and now that she's planted the idea in my mind...."

Bridget stares at me while she processes what I've just said. "Okay, you have a point. I'm just shocked because I didn't think that was something you would even consider. You never talk about anything other than your future goals and being a lawyer, so I just assumed you weren't that interested in dating."

"Well, this isn't a date, so it doesn't count. Zelda's very..." I search my brain for the right word. "Sexual," I finally say, failing to come up with something better. "She's really sexual. It's almost like I can feel it oozing from her."

"Go figure. Dirty Santa." Bridget rolls her eyes and laughs. "What are you going to wear? Or did she ask you to show up in an elf costume or something?"

Now it's my turn to laugh. "I think I'll just wear something like this. She seems to have a thing for the way I dress here."

"Hmm…" Bridget slides off the table, turns to me with a smirk and unbuttons my blouse until my cleavage and half of my bra is visible. "Nice bra. Where did you get that?"

"*Agent Provocateur*, I think." I hold my hand up in protest as she unbuttons it farther, all the way down to my waist, where it's tucked into my skirt. "Hey, what are you doing?"

"Just give me a minute." Bridget ruffles a hand through my hair so it looks messy, pinches the red lipstick I always carry with me from my chest pocket and reapplies a layer before she steps back to inspect me. "There you go."

I chuckle as she fans a hand in front of her face. "Not too much?"

"Hell no. If you're going with the intention of having sex, you might as well embrace the slutty secretary look," she says with a hint of humor. "Even I have to admit that you look very fuckable. If I were into women…"

6

"You came." The woman who opens the door for me looks nothing like the big-bellied Santa at Bergman's, and I need a moment to adjust to the pleasant change in appearance. Zelda is wearing torn jeans and a faded gray Levi's T-shirt, and her short ash-blonde hair is wet and slicked back. Her face is devilishly attractive—now that I can see her strong jawline, her wide smile and her intense blue eyes—her features all working together in harmony without the face paint.

My body reacts to her in crazy ways as she leads the way up the stairs to her studio and lingers behind me way longer than necessary before taking my coat. I like feeling her against my back; it turns me on beyond belief.

"I came," I repeat in a thin voice, wondering what people talk about before they're about to have casual sex. Unfamiliar with the rules, I decide I'm not going to engage in small talk if she doesn't.

Zelda doesn't seem to have a problem with the silence and takes her time picking a bottle of wine from the rack on the kitchen counter, although I don't believe for a minute that she hasn't planned this down to the smallest details. The lighting is just right and soothing music is playing in the background. The cushions on the couch are all resting against one side, and I can tell by the marks on the thick carpet that she's moved the coffee table farther away from it. *Just in case we end up on the couch.*

"Red?" she asks.

"Sure." I nervously shuffle from one foot to the other as I wait for her to open the bottle. It's a little scary to be in a stranger's home, especially with the prospect of getting undressed and doing God knows what. I've only been with a handful of women and I'm not exactly experienced, so I almost changed my mind and turned around on my way here. Not knowing what to expect is nerve-racking and I don't want to disappoint her by being clumsy in bed. Still, I came, knowing I would regret it if I didn't show up tonight. Standing here now—my blouse not quite as unbuttoned as Bridget suggested—I'm kind of proud of myself for taking the step and doing something so bold.

The studio is small but cool, with a dark resin floor, huge windows and gray walls. There's a small kitchen unit with a breakfast bar, and the spacious gray couch and the coffee table are placed in front of the big street-facing windows. Candles are burning on every surface; on the coffee table, the kitchen counter, and on the shelves next to the door. My attention shifts to the king-size mattress that is lying on a base of bare pallets against the back wall at the far end of the room and I feel a stir, knowing I'll be lying in that bed soon. It's made up with natural bedlinen in various shades of white, and next to it is a big, modern, egg-shaped chair with a reading lamp. I'm pleased to see that there are no Christmas decorations in here, apart from the pretty string lights that are hanging on the wall above her bed.

Zelda hands me my wine and I take a sip as I cast my gaze over the photographs on the walls. One of them looks like it's showing Zelda on stage, dressed up like a cat, and there's another one of her and a group of people all wearing similar leather jackets under a blue spotlight.

"Are you an actress?"

"Yes." Zelda comes closer and I can feel her body heat as she clinks her glass with mine and takes a sip. "I've done some TV in the past, but I prefer to be on stage because I love singing and dancing. I've been doing Broadway musicals for the past seven years and this month, I was between jobs. I'm booked to be one of the leads when I join the cast of *Chicago* in January so when my agency offered me the Santa job, I took it." She shoots me a goofy smile. "They were actually looking for a female Santa, believe it or not. You know, diversity and all that; it's important nowadays."

"Hmm. I had no idea businesses asked for female Santas but it makes sense." I look her over and notice her body is seriously ripped. Even through her clothes it's clear that she works out intensely. "So, you're a musical actress on Broadway," I say, rather impressed to learn this about her. "That's so cool."

"Yeah, it's fun." Zelda puts her glass aside and takes mine too. "But there are more fun things in life." Her lips pull into a seductive smile as she leans into me. "Are you ready to have some fun, Lucy?"

"Already?" I expected to at least polish off two glasses of wine before I gave into her advances, but she's moving fast.

"No point in waiting, right? We both know what you're here for."

Unable to answer, I nod slowly. I'm aware that I look like a deer in the headlights and don't want her to think I'm not into her. When she pushes me against the kitchen island, I force myself to relax as there's no going back now.

Everything comes into sharp focus then, as if the touch of her mouth pushes my senses into high alert. I'm aware of the most subtle things; the zingy smell of her shampoo, the trace of mint Chapstick on her lips, her height; she's just a little bit taller than me, the softness of her skin as I reach out to brush my fingertips down her neck, the drum of her quickening heartbeat against my chest that tells me she's just as turned on as I am, and the frenzy of sparks that shoot through every part of me, leaving me breathless.

Her lips feel delicious and when her tongue traces my upper lip, I press my mouth harder against hers, hungry for more. It's impossible to hold back and consumed with lust, I part my lips and sink into the kiss that is slow and sensual and oh so good. Bucking my hips and arching my back in anticipation, I let out a soft moan when she presses her body into mine, filling me with a raging, primal desire. If this kiss is any indication of what's to come, I need to brace myself for sensory overload because I've never been kissed like this. Not with so much purpose and conviction. Zelda kisses not just with her mouth but with her whole body, and the way she holds me and moves into me is intoxicating.

My uncertainties melt like snow and my apprehension evaporates. It's hard to grasp how this has happened but in a matter of seconds I'm passive and relaxed, welcoming her hands that roam all over me. They trace my waistline before she grabs me possessively and holds me like I belong to her.

"Don't be afraid. I just want to make you come really, really hard," Zelda murmurs as she breaks out of the kiss. "That's my thing, you see…"

"Your thing? I like the sound of that." Feeling bolder I drag a finger down her toned arm, shivering as I feel her muscles flex. "But you should never oversell yourself in situations like this. It might lead to disappointment," I add in a teasing tone.

"It won't, I'm pretty confident when it comes to my bedroom skills." Zelda unbuttons my blouse and her gaze darkens as she spots my delicate black lace balcony bra. "What's this?" She licks her lips and tilts her head, parting the white satin fabric to investigate what's underneath. "You're a dark horse, Lucy. I bet I was right about the stockings too." Without warning, she hikes up my skirt and runs her hand over my thigh, her breath hitching when she feels the straps of my garter belt attached to my stockings. They snap back when she pulls at them, leaving a stinging sensation on my thighs. As if she suddenly has trouble controlling herself, her other hand joins in, squeezing my ass hard. "Fuck. That's very sexy. Have you thought about my question?"

"What question?" I ask through ragged breaths. Her firm hand on my behind is incredibly arousing and her eyes have a raw intensity to them that I haven't seen before. I stare into them, hoping she'll see the same reflected in mine.

"Good or bad?"

I chuckle and lick my lips, remembering our conversation in the restrooms. "Since I don't know you... let's go with 'good' for now." For a moment I wonder if she's disappointed with my answer, but then her smile widens and she nods. "Good it is. Are you ready for Santa to give you your reward?"

7

Zelda slips my blouse off my shoulders, and I shudder at the longing I see in her gaze.

"God, you're beautiful," she murmurs, the masterful tone in her voice now gone. She's about to do all kinds of things to me and I have no doubt she knows what she's doing. Her cocky confidence contradicts the sudden tenderness in her touch ever since I've uttered the word 'good', as if she wants to put me at ease before making me explode. It may just be a performance—she's an actress after all—but it's working, and by now I'm pretty sure I'd let her do anything to me. Each caress is electrifying, no matter how light, and the anticipation is building in my core like a fireball.

Zelda's hands slide down my arms as she removes the garment, before they move to my cleavage, tracing the edge of my bra. Her lips are at the nape of my neck, softly kissing my sensitive skin as I close my eyes and tilt my head to one side, leaning farther back against the kitchen counter.

Her skin is smooth under my fingertips as I run my hands under her T-shirt to explore her body, and I feel her tense when I drag my nails down her back. Her handsome face mesmerizes me; she's exactly my type, someone I would pick out of a lineup of a thousand women. A little androgynous, slightly butch perhaps, incredible eyes, sharp bone structure, lush lips that permanently curl up at the corners of her mouth and soft hair to run my fingers through. It's curious that I felt the attraction even with her awful Santa outfit, as if a little voice inside told me we were sexually compatible.

Reaching around me, Zelda continues to kiss her way over my neck and shoulders while she unclasps my bra. Slowly, she slides down the straps and when she steps back, it falls off me, leaving me in my pencil skirt and heels. Her look says it all; she likes what she sees, and I'm aware of my heaving chest as her eyes lower to my small breasts. Her mouth is drawn to my nipples like a magnet, and she runs her tongue over them before sucking one into her mouth.

"Fuck!" With a loud moan, I grab her by the back of her head and pull her closer against me, the twirling of her tongue sending me into bliss. I can feel my panties getting drenched and can't wait for her to touch me where I need it most now. She wasn't underselling herself; it didn't take me long to figure that out. Her hands dance over my body so intuitively, creating a trace of goose bumps in places I didn't even know I liked to be touched while her mouth caresses my breasts that have been neglected for at least a year.

Zelda pulls away from my breasts and looks me over, admiring the hard, glowing buds that have gone a darker shade of nude. She reaches around my waist again to pull down the zipper on my skirt, and I watch her intensely while she does this. I like knowing my body turns her on; there's something very emboldening about feeling desired. Her breath hitches as she slides my skirt down, revealing my black lace panties, my garter belt and the black lace edges of my stockings.

"Keep your heels on," she whispers with a smile. "I love them. I love it all."

I'm shivering but it's not from the cold. Zelda's apartment is warm and inside I'm burning but I've never stood totally brazen in front of someone like this; dressed seductively, in my heels, and exposed. It's thrilling. On the few occasions I've gone home with a woman, we've fallen straight into bed, but Zelda looks like she's going to take her sweet time with me.

"Don't," she says when I wrap my arms around myself, and she takes my hands and leads me to her bed. "You're gorgeous, don't cover yourself up."

I nod and give her a small smile. My eyes dip to her lips and as if on cue, we both lean in to kiss each other again. Wrapping my arms around her, I pull her in to deepen the kiss that grows hungrier by the second. We're both moaning, longing for more and her abdomen tenses against my belly. I have a feeling she may lose control any minute. Tugging at the hem of her T-shirt, I let her know I want to undress her too, and she raises her hands so I can pull it off.

The gray sports bra she's wearing holds firm breasts, at least two sizes bigger than my small handfuls, and my mouth is watering at the thought of exploring them. As if reading my thoughts, she takes the bra off and tosses it on the floor.

My lips part at the sight of her gorgeous torso, and full, inviting breasts with hard nipples that are begging me to wrap my lips around them, but when I reach out to touch her, she shakes her head with a smile.

"Nah-ah. You've been good, so you're getting your reward first, Lucy." The playful way she says it makes me chuckle and I let myself fall on the bed and crawl back when she gestures for me to do so. Laying back in the pillows, I watch her unbutton her jeans and step out of them, leaving her only in a pair of black boxers. My heart is almost beating out of my chest as she crawls onto the bed and straddles me. Feeling a woman's bare skin on mine again is heavenly, but with our undeniable chemistry, it's so intense that it makes me dizzy.

Again, her mouth is drawn to my breasts, devouring them before she kisses me. When she lowers herself on top of me the sensation is almost too much and I'm afraid I might climax from the weight of her body and the sensual kiss alone. Her thigh is between my legs, pushing against my pussy and going on her soft moans, I know she's enjoying this very much. The heat of her body feels wonderful against mine and the tensing of her abs and thigh muscles as she moves into me is making me delirious.

"Spread your legs wider and let me feel how wet you are," she whispers, bringing her hand down between us while she brushes her lips over mine. Our shared breath is flowing between us, and our locked eyes make it all the more intimate. It doesn't feel like my previous flings; it's nothing like that. Although she's practically a stranger, Zelda is not someone I've picked up in a bar after too many drinks. This feels way more real. We're sober and communicating; both with and without words, and our mutual urgent need to please and satisfy each other is stronger than anything I've ever felt before.

I comply, moving my legs apart, and I brace myself for her touch as her hand slips into my panties. As soon as she skims my oversensitive lips, my hips shoot up and I suck in a breath through my teeth. Her fingers feel incredible as they explore my pussy, moving farther down to the pool of liquid that has coated my panties.

"God, you're wet." Zelda smiles against my mouth. "I want to taste you." She moves back and kneels between my legs, then starts releasing the straps of my garter belt. The dark look on her face while she unclips it is incredibly sexy, especially as she never takes her eyes off mine. Lifting my hips, I let her slide down the garter belt along with my panties, and I'm left only in my stockings and heels.

Looking down at my pussy, she licks her lips as if she's just stepped out of a desert in need of a drink. I waxed before I came here, and I'm glad I did now. "Mmm... I like that." Her words are drawn out slowly, followed by a soft moan that makes my core flutter wildly.

I feel exposed and vulnerable but I'm far from uncomfortable. She's put me at ease and when she moves down and runs her tongue over my full length, my hips shoot up again and I cry out in ecstasy. "Fuck!"

"You like that, huh?" she mumbles, taking all of me into her mouth, causing loud moans to escape me. Her skilled tongue moves to my clit, making me jerk up until I'm about to explode. Balancing on the edge, I lace my fingers through her hair, pulling her tight against me as she sucks it into her mouth and does something incredible with her tongue. I come with a force that takes me by surprise and buck against her as she siphons all the pent-up energy out of me, leaving me staring at the ceiling, limp and spent.

"You're incredible," I whisper through heavy breaths as I bring my hands to her cheeks. Feeling her smile, I sit up so I can focus on her, but she pushes me back and pins my hands above my head.

"Not yet."

"What are you doing?" I'm only just coming down from my orgasm, so I don't understand what she wants.

"I'm going to fuck you now," Zelda says in a self-assured, husky voice. "Just like I promised." When she slips two fingers inside me, I'm surprised to feel my body embracing the attention all over again. In fact, it feels even better the second time around and it's thrilling to be filled up by her. Slowly, she starts fucking me, biting her lower lip as she studies my reaction.

"Does that feel good?"

"Yes," I say through ragged breaths, tilting my head from side to side.

"More?"

I'm not sure as no one has ever asked me what I like, so I simply stare up at her, moaning when she pushes into me, a little deeper each time. When her fingers are coated in my juices, she adds a third finger, smiling as I wiggle and squirm. I hold my breath, relaxing into her and when she curls her fingers, it feels so good that I don't know what to do with myself. Zelda lets go of my wrists and I arch my back, fisting the bedsheets.

"Still good?"

"God, yes. Whatever you're doing, don't stop." A ball of fire ignites in my belly and she stops for a moment, making me wait. I shut my eyes tightly and feel her bend over me to rummage through her bedside drawer but I'm too close to care what's happening. When I open them again, I see she's holding a small, pink vibrator.

"You're going to love this," she whispers. Her fingers are still inside me and with a mischievous smile, she continues to fuck me while she turns on the vibrator and places it on my clit. The effect is astonishing, and I come so hard that I lose all control, shifting and bucking against her hand while

I moan loudly. I can hear myself scream in pleasure; there's no way I can be quiet with the waves of intense delight that just keep coming and coming, washing over me like a storm.

I have no idea how long it lasts but it seems like forever and when I slowly come back around, Zelda's smug face is looking down at me. I taste myself on her lips as she kisses me, and I can feel her need as she grinds into me.

"Teach me what you just did," I say, breaking out of the kiss to admire her handsome face. "I want to do that to you."

8

"What do you do for fun?" Zelda throws a piece of fish into the hotpot between us, along with some vegetables and a slice of tofu.

"What do I do for fun?" A frown appears between my brows as I repeat the question, like I have no concept of what 'fun' even means.

The small Chinese restaurant under her studio is chaotic and noisy, and the tables are crammed close together. A chubby chef is shouting orders out from the open kitchen, making the staff jump each time he raises his voice at them. It's a cheerful mess, and the food is excellent. Zelda made good on her promise and took me out for dinner after we'd had a long shower together, and although I feel exhausted, the spicy Szechuan food is making me perk up. I didn't realize how hungry I was until now, and it's exciting to try something new.

"Yeah, fun. You know, food, movies, clubs, bars, music, hobbies... Things that people do besides work," she says with a grin.

"Not much," I finally admit, and wince. "I can't really afford to experience much of the New York nightlife but that doesn't matter. I'm a law student at NYU so I'm generally too busy anyway."

"NYU?" Zelda regards me with interest. "I thought you worked at Bergman's full-time."

"No, I don't think I would last for a year being there full-time, but I get why you thought that as I've practically been there every day over my winter break. I'm studying law at NYU and I work at Bergman's two days a week, normally."

"So you're smart and sexy; that's a very attractive combination." Zelda gives me a stare that turns my insides to mush. Being in her presence makes me feel wanted and that's a wonderful new sensation.

"Not sure I'm that smart, but I work hard, and I'll get there eventually. I only have one more year to go and most of my last year consists of internships so I'm currently working on my applications."

"So, you live on campus?"

"Yeah. One of those tatty, cheap rooms. I share it with Shelley, my roommate."

"Hmm..." Zelda's mind seems to drift elsewhere. "I've always wanted to have sex in a dorm room," she says with a sly smile. "It's a fantasy of mine."

I chuckle. "Didn't you live on campus when you studied drama?"

"No, I lived with my parents as it was only a twenty-minute walk from Tisch."

"Impressive, I've heard Tisch's drama department accepts less than 15 percent of all applicants." I lean in and raise a brow. "Acting prowess aside, I don't believe for one minute that you—the woman who straight-out told me she wanted to fuck me—didn't sneak into other girls' dorm rooms back then."

"Honestly, I didn't." Zelda stirs the broth and scoops some more of the cooked ingredients into my bowl. "I was very focused on my studies and my career. You actually remind me of myself ten years ago."

"Really?" I'm surprised to hear that as Zelda seems like such a carefree spirit. She strikes me as someone who has always done whatever the hell she wants. "What changed?"

"Eight years ago, after doing some commercials and voice-overs whilst auditioning non-stop in L.A., I moved back to New York and got my first gig in an off-Broadway show. It was a small production and it didn't pay much, but I loved it and I met a lot of fun people. Acting in New York is different from acting in Hollywood, and theatre is a whole other world from the movies. Once I found my niche and realized I'd rather be on stage than in front of the camera, the pressure of looking and behaving in a certain manner fell away and I felt like I could finally be myself."

"That makes sense." I'm enjoying getting to know Zelda better, and the more I learn, the more she intrigues me. "So, L.A. wasn't for you?"

"No. I'm a New Yorker through and through. I should have never left in the first place. Don't get me wrong; I love to travel and explore new places. L.A. was a good experience but, in the end, there's no place like home and nothing makes me happier than being on stage." She pauses and hesitates before continuing. "Anyway, I know how it feels to be under pressure and to lead a very singular life with only one goal in mind. I can tell you one thing though; it's not going to make you happy."

"Happy is not what I'm after right now. I can do happy as soon as I pass the bar." I smile. "But tonight has been great."

"It was exceptional and I hope Santa's reward—for you being a good girl—lived up to its billing." Looking me over, Zelda tilts her head and licks her lips. "I hope we can do it again sometime soon."

9

———

"Hey, where were you?" Shelley startles me as I quietly let myself into our dorm room at 1 a.m.

"Jesus, Shelley." Clutching my hand to my chest, I take a couple of deep breaths and lean back against the door. Zelda and I said goodbye outside the restaurant, and I took a cab here. We didn't agree to meet up again and we didn't exchange numbers. There was a kiss though; a long and lingering kiss that left me breathless and longing for more. Looking forward to some private time with my vibrator, as the ache between my legs still hasn't subsided, I'm kind of disappointed to find my roommate here.

"Sorry, Lucy. I didn't mean to scare you. Mom was driving me crazy, so I told her something had come up and that I had to come back here for a couple of days." Shelley wipes her eyes and yawns.

"That's okay. I just didn't expect to see you here." I suppose I was a little on edge to start with, after being out of my comfort zone all night, and after Shelley scaring the crap out of me, my heart is beating out of my chest. "What happened?" I ask, almost tripping over a shoe on the floor. Shelley is back and so is her mess.

"Nothing serious." Her voice is groggy and sleepy. "It's just my mom; she won't stop bugging me about lame Kevin. She's in total denial about the fact that I broke up with him." Shelley turns to me and winces after switching on the lamp on her nightstand. "It's crazy that I'd rather be in a bare dorm room on an empty campus than in my parent's beautiful home over the holidays, but she just goes on and on and I can't take it anymore. I might go back tomorrow; I'll see how I feel."

"Oh, that conversation again." I walk into the bathroom and grab a packet of towelettes, then start removing my makeup as I sit down on my bed. "I thought your mom might have accepted the break-up by now."

"Nah. Same old thing. His parents are loaded so him cheating on me is apparently something that should be forgiven." Shelley yawns. "Anyway, you never answered my question. Where were you? Your schedule said you had an early shift." She points at the worksheet that's taped to the wall above my bed.

"Who are you, the time police?" I chuckle. "I was having dinner with a friend, go back to sleep. We'll talk about your mom in the morning."

Shelley sits up in bed, crosses her legs and brushes a long lock of dark hair away from her pale face. She's wearing a T-shirt with some heavy metal band logo on it and in combination with her nose piercing and her twenty-something ear piercings, she looks nothing like a future lawyer. "Really? Which friend? You don't have any friends apart from me and that co-worker of yours. Sorry, no offence."

"I do have other friends, I just don't go out much," I lie,

then roll my eyes at her. "It's not like you're Miss New York socialite either."

"Touché." Shelley throws her head back and laughs. "Fair enough. Then who was it?"

"Just someone from Bergman's." I kick off my heels and start unbuttoning my blouse, then remember my bra is in my purse and stop what I'm doing. Glancing at the vibrator that's lying on my nightstand in full view, I cringe. Shelley hasn't teased me about it yet, so I suppose she hasn't noticed it's there. "Well, I'm going to have a quick shower before bed. Sorry I woke you up and it's nice to have you back for a while."

"Hey, wait a minute. What's that?" Shelley's probing brown eyes move up toward my neck.

Subconsciously, my fingers caress the sore spot just above my shoulder and I feel my cheeks color. The memory of Zelda sucking at my flesh until it stung makes me twitch, and I'm pretty sure it's obvious by my expression that I'm feeling heated. "It's ehm..." Failing to come up with an explanation, my lips pull into a grin and I shrug. "Come on, you know what it is."

"Fuck me, that must have been some dinner." Shelley gets up and grabs my hand when I'm about to go into the bathroom. "No, no, no, no... You're not going anywhere, Lucy." She reaches for the half-empty bottle of wine on the floor by her bed and takes two red plastic Solo cups from the stack next to it. "We're going to have a drink and you're going to tell me everything."

"Oh God, I don't know," I stammer. "It's late and—"

"Yes, it's late, but this doesn't happen every day. In fact, I don't think I've ever seen you after coming back from a bootie call, and I've always wanted to know what you gay gals get up to in the bedroom."

"Gay gals? Really?" Reluctantly I let Shelley push me back on the bed, then wait for her to pour me a glass of cheap, lukewarm white wine. I don't really feel like drinking after the food and the wine I had earlier. I'm giddy and still on a high from tonight though, and deep down, I do want to talk about it.

"Yeah, I want to hear all about the hot sex that goes on between two women," Shelley adds in a cheeky tone. "So, it's a colleague? Do you have a crush on her? What did she do to you? Is she cute?" Pulling me closer by my arm, she sniffs the air around me.

"Stop that. I smell gross." I panic for a moment, conscious that I really need a shower and that I'm probably infused with the scent of sex.

"Mmm..." Shelley licks her lips and laughs at my red-hot cheeks. "You smell of Chinese food."

10

_____

"What the..." I glance at my tablet again and frown, confused as to what I'm reading. Under client name and address, it says: Santa. Bergman's, ground floor, Santa's sleigh. "This can't be right," I mumble, more to myself than anyone around me. I don't even know what a Fema medium purple is, and it comes with something else I've never heard of either, but the section where I'm supposed to pick it up tells me it's far from innocent.

"What's up, sex kitten?" When Bridget comes over, I quickly scroll to the next order before she can interrogate me further.

"Nothing, I'm great." I check my hair and makeup in the mirror fixed to the door of the gift-wrapping room and straighten my shirt.

"Great," Bridget repeats, arching her brow. "Just great? Are you going to tell me about last night or what?" She blows on her coffee and looks at me over the rim of her cup. "How was your secret Santa meet-up?"

"Not now, I'm super busy." My mouth is not cooperating when I try to suppress a grin and I feel my lips pull into a wide smile. I feel good today. Really good. "Want to have lunch later?"

"Sure. One o'clock okay for you?" She winks. "Let's go for a walk so no one can listen in, shall we? Hot dogs in the park?"

I blow her a kiss. "Sounds good, I'll meet you outside." Still unsure whether Zelda's order is a joke or not, I head out of the break room and cross the enormous upper floor to the 'adult' corner. The area is blocked off by a tall, white wall, and although I've been there a couple of times, it's been at least three months since I last picked up an 'adult' order. I suppose sex toys are not something people would normally buy from a department store; I have a feeling there are websites with a lot more choice out there.

So, Santa wants toys... A flutter runs through me when I read the special request again. Although it's optional, the personal shoppers are not normally specified; no one cares who does the job as long as the right product is delivered on time. Zelda has requested me personally though, which means she wants me to know what she's buying. She'll have to pay thirty percent extra for the personal service and I'm pretty sure she's playing games with me as she could easily just head upstairs and buy what she wants on her break.

"Hey, Lucy. I haven't seen you in a while. What can I help you with?" Connie asks me. Connie is in her late fifties and has worked here for over twenty years. Since the adult section requires a salesperson who is familiar with the products, the department store relies heavily on her as the department manager. She looks far from adventurous in the bedroom department, with her blonde bouffant hairdo and sweet, round glasses, and new employees are always totally startled when she starts talking about sex toys in the break room—usually when they're about to bite into a sub or peel open a banana—as if it's the most common thing in the world. I try to avoid sitting next to her myself, as her conversations make me blush but today, I'm relieved she's on duty.

"Hi, Connie. Glad you're here." I show her the order on my tablet. "I don't know what this is but I'm sure you can help me."

"Absolutely." Connie smiles. "Well that's an excellent choice. She arches a brow and shoots me a knowing look. "Has the client requested anything to go with it?"

"Yes, a *Fema* adjustable harness and a *Fema* battery-operated O-ring." It suddenly clicks when I read it out loud. Curiously, I follow her with my eyes as she walks over to the shelf at the far end of the space and picks up a box. She then heads to the section adjacent to the counter, where a selection of wildly different dildos are mounted to form a jaw-dropping display.

"Here you go," she says nonchalantly, placing the items on the counter before adding another smaller box from the section next to the dildos.

"Thank you." Normally I wouldn't blink an eye, but knowing this is for Zelda, I study the three products with intense curiosity. The first one is a harness, the second a medium-sized purple transparent dildo, and I have no idea what the smaller box contains. It looks like a silicone ring of some sort, with a lead and a remote. Other than the product image, the box gives nothing away about its use. I want to ask Connie what it is but I'm not comfortable with conversations like this. Possibly a little bored herself as the department is deserted today, Connie starts rambling off a pitch about the pros and cons of each item like she's trying to convince me to get one for myself.

"That's a vibrating device," she says, pointing to the small box after educating me on the practicalities of the strap-on that is apparently award-winning in its category. For a hundred-and-eighty dollars, it better be. "You pull it around the shaft, and it stimulates the clitoris of both you and your partner. It's really quite thrilling." Then Connie's eyes widen as if she's suddenly had a light bulb moment. "Oh, this lube is on offer this week." She hands me a tube from the counter. "Perhaps you'd like to call your client and suggest we add this to the order?"

As I try to come up with an excuse as to why I don't have a number, I change my mind and smile. If Zelda's playing games with me, I might as well give her the full package. "You know what? That's a great suggestion. This client trusts me so there's no need to call her. I'm sure she'll be delighted if you just add it on." I'm aware of my flustered state and glance down at my feet. "Do you have a bag for me?"

"Of course." Connie pulls a discrete white bag from underneath her counter and carefully places the items inside while I fill in the order details and proof of payment for her records. "Anything else I can help you with, dear? Something for yourself, perhaps? There's nothing wrong with treating yourself for Christmas."

Again, I shake my head and take a step back. "No, I'm good, thanks." Is it that obvious, or can she smell that I have sex on my mind? "Well, have a lovely day," I stammer, taking the bag from her. On shaking legs, I leave the 'adult' corner and run right into the staff restrooms. Steadying myself against the sink, I'm shocked to see the redness on my neck and cheeks. I look like I've just come out of a sauna and it's not exactly warm in here. I splash some cold water on my face and almost forget the bag as I leave. Zelda's requested the items are wrapped in pink paper with an orange ribbon, which is a ridiculous combination, so I assume she's just randomly ticked a couple of boxes to finish her order.

With anyone else I would carry out the request, but as it's for her, I decide to wrap it up with great care and choose the materials I like best to make the presents look spectacular. I'm relieved to be alone in the gift-wrapping room and start off with gold paper with a matt finish for the big box and the same gold paper with a shiny finish for the smaller ones. Using gold ribbon, I create a bouquet-like centerpiece on the top of each item, with faux gold twigs, origami roses and beads nestled in between. The result is beautiful and just for fun, I draw a smiley face on the box containing the lube.

Deciding now is not the right time to deliver the goods —as Santa's stage will be filled with children—I place the items in my locker before I carry on with the rest of my orders. If Zelda's trying to shake me up, she's certainly succeeded.

11

As I approach Santa's stage, I'm surprised to see that there are still three children gathered around Zelda. A young ginger-haired boy sits beside her while two girls stand on either side of her, gawking up at her in adoration. Their parents are waiting next to the stage and look pretty engaged too.

When I realize it's Friday, I mutter a quiet curse. As I often work past opening hours, I sometimes lose track of what day it is, especially during busy periods and holidays when I don't have any exams to focus on. Tonight, we don't close until ten, but even so, eight p.m. seems a little late for such young children to be in a department store. Zelda leans forward, whispers something to them, and the children's eyes widen with excitement. Before I have the chance to walk away again, she spots me and calls me over.

"Children, this is Lucy," she says to the kids, using her low Santa voice. "Lucy works at Bergman's. She's been a very good girl, but she's a little shy around Santa. Why don't you come over here, Lucy!"

"You don't need to be shy!" one of the little girls shouts

from the top of her lungs. "Santa is nice. He gave me candy and he says I'll get presents." She waves a fistful of candy at me. "And he took my letter with my wish list," she says, making me laugh.

"He did?" I ask, smiling at her. "Well, then you must have been a good girl too."

"That's right. Tamieca has been on her best behavior this year." Zelda holds up a piece of paper before she drops it into a box next to her that says, *'Letters to Santa'*. "Come closer, Lucy. There's really no need to be shy."

I should be annoyed that's she's using the kids as a means to get me over there, but I have to admit that she's kind of sweet and all kinds of funny in her role. As I look at the children, I realize that I am in fact feeling shy with three pairs of eyes fixed on me, plus their parents staring in my direction. "I have a delivery for Santa," I say, holding up the bag. *That will teach her,* I think to myself as I hand over the unobtrusive package. There's no way she can open it here in front of the kids and their parents.

"A delivery for me?" Zelda asks in a dramatic voice, never stepping out of her role. She places her hand on her heart and smiles at me. "How wonderful. Santa usually doesn't get presents himself."

"Open it!" the boy beside her says while he picks his nose.

Zelda hesitates, then shakes her head. "Even Santa can't open his presents until Christmas Day. That wouldn't be right now, would it?" She pauses while all three kids nod in agreement, then taps her knee. "But you know what? You've all told Santa what you'd like for Christmas, now let's ask Lucy what she'd like. Lucy, why don't you come and sit on Santa's lap?"

"She's a grown-up. She can't sit on your lap." The boy chuckles, and his parents look amused too.

"Oh yes, she can. Even grown-ups like presents, don't they?" Zelda winks at his parents. "Your mom might be up next." Her banter leads to hilarity among the kids, and I can see the boy's mother blush. Apparently, I'm not the only one who's got her eye on Santa.

"I'm a little busy, Santa," I say with a shrug, but give in when the children insist. My pulse starts racing when I sit down on her lap sideways and try my best to stay composed when she pulls me further in.

"So, Lucy. We've already established that you've been a good girl this year," Zelda says in a teasing tone.

"Of course," I say with a smirk that widens when I meet her blue eyes.

"Are you sure about that? Because Santa's helpers see everything, you know." Her hand moves to my thigh so subtly that I'm sure no one notices, but the fire that flares up inside me is hard to hide.

"Yes. I'm always good." My matter-of-fact tone leads to more hilarity from the kids and the parents, but little do they know—it's kind of true.

"That's what Santa likes to hear." Zelda makes a come-hither motion with her index finger, then points to her ear. "Since you don't have a wish list with you, why don't you whisper to Santa what you would like for Christmas?"

Suppressing an eye roll, I let out a chuckle and feel my temperature rise even more as I lean in and place my mouth against her ear, covering it with my hands. Feeling bolder now and wanting to get back at her, I whisper, "I'd like to know what you're planning on doing with those toys you've ordered."

I feel Zelda's body shake with amusement, and know

she's trying to stop herself from laughing. "I'm sorry, I'm not sure if I heard that right. Did you say something about toys?" Her fake, white bushy brows shoot up when the boy's mom bursts out in laughter. "Aren't you a little old for toys?"

"Yes, you're right, Santa. I'm too old for toys," I say, holding up a hand in defeat. I'm not going to win this one, so I might as well give up trying to beat her at her own game.

"Well how about this then..." Zelda pauses for dramatic effect. "How about Santa surprises you?"

"Yes!" the boy yells, leaping from his seat to jump up and down as if Zelda's talking about his own presents. "And then he'll come through the chimney and bring it to your house."

"And he'll put it in your stocking," one of the girls adds. "And then you get candy too."

"That sounds exciting," I say, casting my gaze over the tiny humans. I think their parents know there's a bit of flirtation going on between Santa and myself, but they don't seem to mind. "In that case, I would love a surprise." Getting up, I playfully slap away Zelda's hand that's about to move to my behind and smile over my shoulder before I walk off. "I'll see you soon then, Santa."

12

Never have I looked forward to my shift as much as today, and I notice I'm walking with a bounce in my step as I enter Bergman's through the staff entrance. It's 7:30 a.m. and they're not open yet, but the carols are already blasting through the sound system, the thousands of string lights and other electronic decorations are switched on, and the smell of baked cinnamon buns is wafting from the bakery counter. It always reminds me of a circus this time of year, but I suppose it is all about the theatre. People come here to be seduced and Bergman's is one of the best in the art of seduction. Anything is sellable if marketed and presented the right way, even the hideous illuminated elves that are staged around a light installation in the Christmas department.

Despite the early hour, I'm wide awake, and my heart starts racing when I spot Zelda, who is setting up her stage for the day. She's in her Santa outfit and after the other night it's hard to imagine that I ever assumed she was a man. Unsure of what to do, I linger by the jewelry counter for a beat, then decide to walk past her on my way to the elevators as it would be awkward not to say hello again. I thought about her a lot last night and wouldn't mind repeating our rendezvous.

"Lucy." Zelda pushes her Santa hat up and shoots me a wink when I approach her. "It's good to see you again." She steps off her stage where she's arranging presents in playful piles and comes so close that we almost touch. "Did you manage to catch up on sleep? I never got the chance to thank you for the other night; I had a really good time." She pauses and going by the lust-filled expression in her eyes, I know exactly what's going on in her mind. I feel her breath on my lips and fight the urge to kiss her as I remember the sensation of her mouth on mine. And her mouth exploring other places too.

"Hey." I clear my throat and try to stay composed. "I did, and thank you. It was fun."

"That's what I like to hear." Pressing her big Santa belly against mine, she subtly runs her finger over my lower arm, causing me to shiver.

I have to ask the question that's been burning on my mind since yesterday, simply because I've been able to think of little else. "Did you unwrap your toys?" I sound nervous as the words leave my mouth and I hate the high pitch in my voice. I've been wondering if she has a lot of girlfriends, and the thought of her fucking someone else annoys me, so I have to know. Not that she owes me anything; we never made any promises, but I've noticed I've taken a real interest in her. I'm not looking for commitment—quite the opposite in fact—but I don't like to share either.

"Toys? What toys?" she asks in an innocent tone, clearly sensing I'm a little prudish about these things.

"Come on, you know what I mean," I say, shifting from one foot to the other as I look around to make sure none of my colleagues are listening in. "The items in your personal delivery; the ones I so kindly dropped off yesterday."

"Oh those..." Zelda smirks. "The ones you wrapped in the wrong color paper. I might have to put you on the naughty list for that. Yes, I did open my presents, but I haven't played with them yet. I did bring them though, I thought I'd share them with someone special." When she stares at me, the ball of fire in my lower belly expands and goes wild. "What time's your break?"

My cheeks flush as I stare at her. "I'm off at one. Why?"

"Because Thursday night made me hungry for more and I'd like to have you for lunch today." Zelda steps back, and I let go of the breath I've been holding. She walks over to the large chalk board next to the stage that announces what times Santa will be there. It says: *'9-12:30,' and below: '13:30-18:00.'*

I laugh when she wipes the information away and changes it to *'09:00-13:00' and 14:00-18:00.'* "Can you just do that?"

"I don't see why not." Zelda shrugs and meets my eyes, no doubt picking up on every emotion that runs through me. Arousal, excitement, curiosity, anticipation... "Meet me in the utility room on the sixth floor." She rummages through her pocket and holds up a key. "It's where I keep my Santa stuff; I can lock it from the inside." When I don't answer, she lowers her voice. "Come on, Lucy. I know you want to." Then she adds in a whisper: "I'm wearing something special for you."

I gasp as she takes my trembling hand and brings it between her legs, where I feel something long and hard. "Jesus, Zelda!" I jump back and look around, wide-eyed. There are a dozen or so co-workers near, but everyone is minding their own business, getting their stations ready and preparing for the day ahead. Knowing she's wearing the strap-on for me causes wetness to pool between my legs, and I'm sure she can see how turned on I am. My chest is heaving as my gaze lowers to her crotch, worried it might be visible but it's not. The Santa outfit is loose, and anyway, her fake belly is hanging too low to show anything.

"Sorry. Too presumptuous?" Without even a hint of regret, Zelda bites her lip and shrugs. "If you're not into that, just tell me. I'll take it off."

I'm too stunned to get a word out, and my eyes won't stop flickering back and forth between her face and her crotch. "No, I like it," I finally say, going on the way my body is reacting to the idea. No one has given me a physical high like she has, and I'm so drawn to her that I've lost all control. I attempt to steer my mind toward something else—anything—to stop myself from squirming. "I think."

"You think?" She arches a brow in surprise. "You mean you've never been fucked with a strap-on?"

"No. I haven't been with that many women and the ones I've slept with were kind of conservative in the bedroom," I mumble quietly. Sex has never been about the orgasm for me; no woman has ever given me one apart from Zelda and toys were certainly never in the picture. It was more about feeling a warm body against my own, and about assuring myself everything still worked.

Zelda changed that last night; she's shown me that sex can be mind-blowing, and I'm afraid that after my first hit, I'm already addicted. I glance around again, a little nervous to be having this saucy conversation with her in public. Bridget is just turning the corner from one of the perfume booths and when she spots us, she giggles, then stares shamelessly. In return, I glare at her and nod to the higher floors, letting her know I'll be in the gift-wrapping room soon. Then I turn back to Zelda, mystified as to how she's got me so hooked on her, and most of all, why she's gotten me so adventurous and curious. Gone are my thoughts of application letters and exams. Instead, my mind is filled with juicy fantasies, and they all involve her. "I have to go," I say, checking my watch. "I'll see you at one."

13

The morning has been a waiting game, and I've been unable to keep my thoughts under control. Utterly distracted and drowning in both nerves and anticipation, both my hands are clamping around the big coffee mug I'm carrying with me in an attempt to look like I'm on an innocent break. Sneaking into the quiet corridor that leads to the utility room, I see the door is ajar. *Is she in there? Or is it one of the cleaners?* I feel for our team of cleaners, who have been made to dress up as elves this month but at least I can spot them from a mile away in their hideous bright green costumes. I doubt any of them will be here at this time though, as the second shift has just started.

Holding my breath, I peek inside before I step into the dark room, then exhale deeply when I see a Santa silhouette only a few feet away from me. Zelda comes closer and smiles as she pulls down her beard and throws her wig and hat on the floor. Wasting no time, I close the door and turn the key in the lock before I kiss her, simultaneously running a hand across the wall to find the light switch.

Zelda pushes me against the door just as I flip the

switch, and she kisses me back like we've been separated for months—not mere hours—like she's been starving for me. It's delicious and moreish and so sexy. When I realize that the moans cutting through the silence are coming from me, I'm already worried about making too much noise. As she pulls out of the kiss and runs a hand through my hair, I allow myself to drown in her eyes for a moment and reality hits me. I have a huge crush on this woman who has somehow managed to get me into the utility room on my lunch break to do very, very naughty things with her.

My hands roam under her fur-lined red jacket to find warm skin, and I feel her shiver as I run my nails along her back and pull her in closer. Lust is a strange thing; it makes me irresponsible and carefree and so, so greedy. The greed is mutual, as Zelda has tugged my blouse up to my waist and pulled down my panties in a matter of seconds. Knowing what she's wearing, I'm incredibly wet, and I want her to take me exactly as she pleases.

Zelda does just that; lifting me up and perching me on top of one of the industrial washers beside the door. The surface feels cold against my skin and the edge of the bucket on top is digging into my back, but it only adds to the excitement of this raw encounter.

"I can't wait to fuck you again," she whispers, spreading my legs and stepping between them. A hint of devilry is flashing in her eyes; the same look I saw on Thursday night, and I can feel her need in her strong hands squeezing my thighs.

I wrap my legs around her hips, and she unbuttons my blouse far enough to slip her hand inside and squeeze my breasts and my nipples until they're rock-hard. While we fall into another heated kiss, she takes something out of her pocket and fumbles with it. She brings her hand between my legs, and I gasp at the cold sensation against my pussy. "What are you doing?"

"You know what it is; you took the naughty liberty to add it to my order," she whispers against my mouth. "Good choice, Lucy. Trust me, you'll like it."

Zelda's right; I do like it very much and as the gel adjusts to my body temperature, I jerk my hips against her hand and surrender to the slippery and glowing sensation it arouses. She rubs me in slow, circular motions while she claims my mouth but I need her to stop or I'll climax too quickly.

"I've been imagining this moment all morning," she says, and from the look on her face, I believe her. "You have no idea how sexy you look on top of that washer," she adds with a grin before pulling down her red pants, then lowering her boxers.

I stare at the purple strap-on I picked up for her and swallow hard. Even though it's not the first time I've seen the product, it looks a little more daunting when she's wearing it. My pussy is twitching for attention, but it seems larger than it did in the packaging.

"I'll be careful," she whispers and guides it between my legs. She slides it up and down between my lips until I'm squirming and begging for her to take me. The lube and her foreplay have made my pussy swollen and wet, glowing with a subtle heat and I'm so turned on that I simply can't wait any longer.

"Please," I whisper with pleading eyes as I lace my fingers through her hair, pressing my forehead against hers. "Please fuck me."

Zelda's gaze is filled with an insatiable fire as she pushes the dildo inside me little by little while she kisses me hard and digs her nails into my thigh. It feels like it's too much at first, but then I get used to its girth and need more. Shifting toward the end of the washer, I lean back to take it deeper, moaning as I wrap my arms around her neck and push my hips into her. "That feels good," I mumble, loving the full sensation it gives me.

She hooks her arm under my knee and wraps her other hand around my back to steady me, then starts fucking me slow and deep, sending us both into a heady trance of passion. Her eyes are hazy now, the frown between her brows prominent as she grinds all the way into me, seeking release herself from the friction it gives her. I pull her in to kiss me and move along with her, faster, harder, locked together by our hips and our hungry mouths. It's intense, and I feel beads of sweat dripping down my back and dampness on Zelda's skin as I grab her by the back of her neck. She's close, I can hear it in her ragged breathing and feel it in the frantic way she's moving now. I'm close too—the washer is rocking in time with her thrusts, the dildo glistening with my juices as she plunges into me again and again—and I try to wait but it's impossible to stop the roaring climax that's about to send me to greater heights.

"Come," she whispers, sensing my need. Zelda covers my mouth with her hand as I cry out, stifling the noise and the echoes in the bare room. Orgasmic spasms take over my entire body, engulfing my senses. I feel my walls frantically clamping around the still buried shaft as my vision turns white and all I can do is hold onto her and be in the moment. Only seconds later, Zelda starts shaking and explodes too, but she fails to be quiet. Roaring moans leave her beautiful lips, then soft whimpers of pleasure that make my heart sing with joy. The moment is somehow incredibly intimate and it even feels romantic in some weird way, even though we're fucking on top of a grimy washer in a badly lit utility room.

The sound of a key as someone attempts to enter the room pulls us back to reality, and I'm unable to hold back another moan as she pulls out of me. Quickly slamming a hand in front of my mouth, I stare at the door. Someone's trying to open it but Zelda's key is in the lock.

"Who's in there?" A man yells. "Open the damn door."

14

_____

"**A**m I interrupting something?" The cleaner asks, his eyes narrowing as they dart from Zelda to me and back. Shoving his mop bucket cart inside, he looks furious as he closes the door behind him. I can't help but chuckle as he's dressed as an elf and that makes him an angry elf. Also, his pants and jacket are a little on the short side and with his tall and skinny pale frame, it does him no favors. "Why was the door locked?"

Zelda has her back turned to him, adjusting her costume and putting away the strap-on. When she turns around to face him, her faux fur-lined red jacket is buttoned up, the wide, black belt is tightened snug under her fake belly, and she's pulled up her pants, straightened her beard and adjusted her hat and wig like nothing ever happened. "Well, if it isn't Andy the Elf," she jokes in her Santa voice, and I chuckle, relieved she's fallen into her role flawlessly, drawing the attention away from me while I subtly straighten my skirt and blouse. "Of course you're not interrupting, Andy. I was just helping this lovely lady here find some paper towels to clean a coffee spillage in the gift-wrapping room.

I'm impressed that Zelda knows the cleaner by name; even I don't know them all after three years here and hearing her say his name seems to calm Andy down a little. I don't get why he's so worked up in the first place, but some people are just naturally grumpy and perhaps he is one of those people.

"Well, Santa," he says, playing along. "The paper towels are over there, although this young lady should have some in her room too." He points to a pile of paper towels on one of the shelves behind us, then turns to me. "I'll refill your box if you're out. Or I could head up there and clear it up for you?" He puts down his bucket, clips the mop off his stick and throws it into the very same washer that I was having my brains fucked out on less than a minute ago.

"No, that's not necessary, I'm sure you're busy enough," I'm quick to say, and cringe when he wipes a finger over a blob of lube that seems to have spilled during our flash of passion. A translucent trail is slowly dripping down the side of the washer.

"Okay. Just don't hesitate to give me a shout next time; it's what we're here for and if management sees personal shoppers cleaning their own stations, they'll assume we're not doing our jobs properly," Andy the Elf says absently while studying the gel. "What the fuck is this?" He brings his finger to his nose and when he can't detect any smell, he shrugs, grabs a paper towel and wipes it off. Just when I think we've gotten away with it, he shifts his attention back to me and points at my blouse. "I suggest you take care of that before you go back out there."

I look down and see that in my panicked rush, I've buttoned my blouse up wrong; I've skipped one button in the middle and along with my tousled hair, I literally look like I've been doing exactly what I've just been doing. "Oh, thank you. I can't believe I've walked around like this all morning," I say in an attempt to smooth it over.

"Bullshit." Andy takes a clean mop out of the laundry dryer next to the washer, clips it onto the handle and walks over to the sink to empty his bucket. "I know what you two have been up to," he continues with a sarcastic chuckle. "Imagine what HR would say if they hear Santa and the cute personal shopper have been getting it on in the utility room."

There's no point in denying it; I think our flushed faces say it all. I don't know Andy personally, but I've heard he loves to gossip and that he's reported colleagues before. "But you won't tell them, will you?" I say, glaring at him.

"Hmm..." Andy pretends to think about that, rubbing the stubble on his chin while he patiently waits for his bucket to fill. When it's full, he places it back onto the cart and pushes it away so it rolls toward the door to block our exit, all the while leaving us in an awkward silence. "I might be able to keep it to myself, if there's something in it for me," he finally says, putting on an elf voice that makes him seem even creepier than he already is.

"That's blackmail, Andy." I study him for signs of banter, but he's serious and I feel anger welling up. It's very rare that I lose my temper; three years of court practice have taught me to always stay composed and although I'd very much like to shove that dirty mop into his mouth, I remain calm as I don't want to make matters worse by pissing him off.

"Sure." He shrugs and pouts his thin lips. "What are you going to do about it?"

"This is ridiculous." Zelda rolls her eyes. "I can't believe we're even having this conversation." She stands tall, crosses her arms in front of her chest and shoots him a warning look. "Frankly I don't care if you report me to HR, but I don't want Lucy to get in trouble."

"No one will get in trouble." Andy takes the same stance, mimicking her body language. "As I said, as long as I get something out of it, we're good." It looks like they're having a Mexican stand-off and if I wasn't so furious with him, I would have laughed at Santa standing in the middle of the room arguing with an elf.

I take a step toward him, joining team Zelda. "You can't prove a thing. It's your word against ours."

"Are you sure about that?" Andy points to the far corner of the room and I freeze when I spot the security camera, discreetly placed between bottles of bleach on top of the shelving unit.

Panic, dread and shame hit me all at once. Has the security guard been watching us? I will never be able to look him in the eyes again. "Did you know about that?" I ask Zelda.

"Of course not!" she looks just as shocked as I am, and her face turns pale while she scratches her white curly wig.

"We've had employees stealing from this room over the past year, so I suggested to management they install a camera," Andy says smugly. "No one ever checks them unless something goes missing and they tape over the footage after seventy-two hours. But if I were to tell them I've seen suspicious activity in here, they'd go through them. Not sure how long you were in here before I caught you but from the state of you both, my guess is you've been in here a while." He laughs. "That's going to be some X-rated movie."

Zelda lets out a sigh of defeat, but I can see her hands are balled into fists and for a moment, I'm worried she's going to punch him. "Okay. What do you want?"

"I want to be 'Employee of the Month'," Andy says in all

seriousness. "Not in January, but this month. Management will be voting on the candidates in three days' time so use that time wisely to influence their decision."

"What? I can't make that happen." Zelda raises her voice. "I'm not even employed by Bergman's."

"You're Santa, aren't you? Figure something out." The bells on Andy's green shoe-covers jingle as he trotters over to his cart and leaves without another word.

Zelda turns to me after he's closed the door and we stare at each other for long moments. "Did that just happen?" she asks incredulously.

As the recent developments sink in, I'm not sure whether to laugh or cry. His elf outfit, the lube, his preposterous demand... "I thought he was going to ask for money or something."

"Yeah, me too." Zelda opens the door for me as we leave. "I'm sorry, this is my fault. The thing with Andy is personal. We have the same agent and he was jealous that I got the Santa gig; he's been making snarly remarks at me. I had no idea he worked here as a cleaner before I started. Perhaps acting jobs have been thin on the ground for him."

"Andy's an actor?"

"Yeah. A frustrated one. He had a minor role in a play I was part of a couple of years back, but I never saw him until we met here again."

"It's not your fault that he holds a grudge against you," I say, squeezing her hand. "I am seriously worried about that tape, though. Losing my job is one thing but what if one of those security guards decides the footage is too good to erase? I can't risk a sex tape being released on some seedy website." I pause as worst-case scenarios flash before me. My future employers seeing it, the opposition using it to cut deals, my mother seeing it... "It's not just me. Your career is at stake here too; your agent could drop you for having sex on the job."

"Yeah. Looks like we're both in trouble," Zelda mumbles. "Do you know the security team? Any chance you could talk one of them into erasing it right away?"

"No. I don't know them, and I don't want to point out something they're not aware of." I groan. "Fucking Andy. I don't get why being Employee of the Month is so important to him. There's not even a bonus involved."

"My guess is he just loves being the center of attention. I could tell management that he saved a child from choking or something..." Zelda says, thinking out loud.

"You're right, we could just make something up." I let out a long, frustrated sigh. "Well, we have three days to come up with a solution."

"Yes, but the sooner we solve this the better." I think we should talk about this and carefully consider our options. Come for a drink with me tonight."

"Okay..." I walk with her to the staff elevator, even though I'm not going down myself. She's right. We have to solve this quickly or I'll have sleepless nights and quite possibly a nervous breakdown.

Zelda pushes the button to the ground floor. "There's this bar just off Broadway where actors hang out after their shows. I think you might like it." She shoots me a flirty smile and even through my anxiety, it turns my insides to mush. "And if you're up for it, we could go to my place after. I really enjoyed earlier, and I wouldn't mind doing it again, taking my time."

"I enjoyed it too," I whisper, returning her playful look. I don't know how it's possible but even after being busted and blackmailed, I still have sex on my mind. "You drive me crazy; you know that?" My clit is still throbbing, and I have this pulsing ache between my legs that can only be soothed by more of her. More sex. Zelda has a hold on me.

"Do I?"

The elevator doors ping as they open, and I hold my hand in place to stop them from closing. Tilting my chin up, I brush my lips over hers. "I'll come and find you downstairs after work."

15

Zelda's go-to bar is tucked away in a dark alley in the theatre district. I would never have found this on my own and it's clearly a well-kept secret. The drinks menu is simple, and the interior is old and a little rough around the edges, with chipped tables covered in candle wax, worn-out barstools, and ragged red velvet curtains to either side of the small stage where a solo artist has just finished his gig for the night. He was very talented, and I've enjoyed sitting here with her, listening to him sing over beers. The lights are dimmed to the minimum and although it's a busy Saturday night, the vibe is very chilled. When I went to the restrooms earlier, I was surprised to see a bunch of actors I recognized from a sitcom, gathered around one of the tables in the back. They were dressed low-key, in jeans and hoodies, playing cards with a bottle of tequila between them.

Zelda knows the staff and most of the patrons. She introduced me to everyone who came over for a chat, and they all seemed warm and fun. It's interesting to see her in her own environment with like-minded people, and I note that while she blends in seamlessly, dressed down in jeans and a navy blue sweater, I look highly out of place here, still in my work attire and high heels. Even if I wanted to blend in, I don't have anything suitable in my wardrobe but I know Zelda likes the way I dress and that's enough to make me feel confident.

"So, what kind of law are you planning on specializing in?" she asks when the musician puts away his guitar and steps off the stage. "Intellectual property? Criminal?"

"I want to be a divorce lawyer," I say without hesitation. "And I want to be the best."

"What?" A grimace settles over Zelda's face. "Are you serious?"

"Yeah. Why is that so weird to you?"

"I don't know. It sounds a little depressing, for one. Helping to end marriages…"

My mouth falls open as she utters the words that are quite frankly, a little insulting. "Oh my God, don't tell me you're one of those hopeless romantics who believe love lasts forever." I wait for her reply, but she just stares back at me. "Really? You think divorce is wrong?"

Zelda takes her time before she answers my question. "I don't think it's wrong," she finally says. "But I do think people don't try hard enough these days. Life isn't plain sailing and anyone who believes marriage is easy is naïve, but that doesn't mean you should just give up."

Narrowing my eyes at her, I take a sip of my beer. "Maybe. But you shouldn't judge; some people don't have a choice." Realizing I sound a little sharp, I force myself to relax. "Anyway, what do you care what kind of law I practice? It's not like we'll see each other again after Christmas."

"Oh, really?" Zelda looks surprised. "Why not?"

Now it's my turn to be silent as I hadn't expected that answer. This was supposed to be a one-night stand, nothing more. But here we are, three days later and I'm still enjoying our time together. "Well, for one, this has literally just been about sex. There's nothing romantic about it." I shrug. "It's a hook-up and that's what people do after a hook-up. They move on."

"But it's a good hook-up, isn't it? We could do it again..." Zelda's carefree expression is back as she squeezes my thigh, giving me that intense stare that sends butterflies through every part of me. "And again, and again..." She pauses. "Besides, I find you interesting and I'd like to get to know you better, so consider this our first date."

"A date..." I frown and bite my lower lip as I consider that.

"Don't panic, no strings." Zelda chuckles at my startled expression. "Come on, Lucy. There's nothing wrong with getting to know each other."

"I'm not sure if I want to tell you more after your reaction when I told you I wanted to be a divorce lawyer." My smile is playful, but my tone challenging. I don't hold it against her though; I get that reaction from everyone.

"I'm sorry. I shouldn't have said that." Zelda places a hand on her heart and juts out her bottom lip. "Will you please forgive me and tell me more about yourself?"

"Okay..." I chuckle at her dramatic gesture and try to think of something interesting to tell her but there's not much to my life at the moment. If she was put off by my career ambitions, then she'll be even more disappointed by my boring background. "This is me; I'm hardworking, highly ambitious, super motivated and I should probably learn to let go a little more. I have a thing for pretty lingerie. It's the only thing I splurge on. I've done odd jobs since I was fifteen and spent most of my younger years cleaning cars, babysitting, mowing lawns and walking dogs to help my mother pay the bills. After that I worked in stores, call centers and even at a funeral home before Bergman's employed me three years ago, when I got into NYU. My background is working class—there's nothing artistic about me—although I do play a little piano. I taught myself when Shelley went through a musical phase and got a keyboard for our room. She never used it herself and it broke last year when someone spilled a drink over the keys so that was the end of my musical phase."

"But you enjoyed playing?"

"Yes, I enjoyed it very much. I think I'll get a portable keyboard once I've got my own place. I seriously can't wait to move away from campus. Don't get me wrong," I quickly add. "Shelley is lovely, but I could really do with some privacy now. I grew up living in a small studio with my mother and after that, I lived in a dorm room, so I've never really had any space to myself."

"That sucks. What about your father? Is he around?"

"He's dead to me," I simply say, then decide to change the subject as this is getting a little too personal. I feel no pain or sadness when I think about him, just a flash of the familiar anger, and I don't want to ruin our night by talking about him.

"I'm sorry to hear that." Zelda visibly flinches and sensing the topic is off-limits, she changes the subject. "Maybe we should stick to our plan and discuss what on earth we're going to do about Andy the blackmailing elf. I've thought about it today and it's unlikely that my agency would drop me as I've just signed a six-month contract. They wouldn't want to miss out on their commission, but you might lose your job and that's what worries me most."

"I've thought about it too," I say, grateful for the turn in the conversation. "If you agree, I don't think we should let him blackmail us. I spoke to Bridget and she says the security guys are decent people, so I'll just have to trust that they won't leak the video." I shrug. "And if this is the end of my career at Bergman's, then I'll just have to make sure I find another job immediately. The job market is pretty buoyant at the moment and I'm super employable so if I'm lucky, it won't be a disaster."

"Super employable?" Zelda laughs. "That's a big statement."

"I am." To prove my point, I take up my interview position, straightening my back and lowering my hands calmly into my lap. Then I paint on my friendliest, most sympathetic smile and lean in toward her, raising my voice just a notch as I speak in an animated girl next door tone. "It's always been a dream of mine to work here. At Bergman's, Christmas just seems so..." I let out a deep sigh and raise my eyes skyward, fluttering my lashes. "Magical."

"That's impressive." Zelda shakes with laughter and gives me a thumbs-up. "Is that how you got the job?"

"Yup. It's always worked for me. I never once got turned down after an interview." I wink. "Actors aren't the only ones who act, you know. Lawyers need some talent on that front too. The courtroom is like a theatre, in a way."

"I get that," Zelda says, regarding me with interest. "Have you been acting with me?"

"No. Have you? You're the real talent when it comes to acting."

"You don't know that, you've never seen me on stage," she retorts with a cheeky smile, leaning in on her elbow and resting her chin in the palm of her hand.

"True." I lean in too, mimicking her relaxed body language. "But I've seen you at Bergman's and you're pretty damn good at pretending to be Santa. It's not just the kids who love you; the parents seem hugely entertained too."

"You've been watching me?" she asks.

"You know I have."

"You're right, I've seen you on the ground floor an awful lot lately." Zelda runs a hand over my thigh. "But to answer your question; no, I haven't been acting with you. I genuinely like you a lot." She moves back again when she sees the panicky expression on my face. "Oops. Too much? You seem terrified of anything beyond sex. Do you have some serious issues I should know about?"

I shake my head and laugh because Zelda seems to say all the right things every time I get jittery. "No, I like you too. I'm just not used to this," I say pointing between us.

"To dating?" she asks, arching a brow at me.

"Yes. I guess I've learned from a very young age not to rely on anyone but myself. So that's what I've been doing; it's always been just me. And my mom," I add. "We're a team."

"Are you close to her?"

"Yes, we're very close but I only see her about once a week nowadays. We both have busy lives; me with studying and work, and my mother with her two jobs."

"Where does she work?" Zelda asks.

"She's a waitress at a diner and she also works as a cleaner in a hotel two mornings a week. My mother's a hard worker, always has been. She's always had to be I suppose, since..." I stop myself there as again, this feels like it's getting way too personal. "Never mind. What about your parents?"

"They live in New York and we're close too," Zelda says. "But they're currently in Europe, exploring the continent in an RV so I haven't seen them in a while. They were supposed to be back by now but changed their minds and are staying for another two months."

"That sounds like a nice life."

"Yeah, well, they're old hippies." Zelda grins. "A conventional life is not for them; they do whatever the hell they want." She finishes her beer. "Do you want another drink? Or are you hungry? It's nine-thirty and we didn't have much to eat apart from those cookies after work."

"I could eat." I'm actually really hungry now and the two beers I've had are going to my head. "Any suggestions?"

"Why don't you decide. Is there somewhere you'd like to go?"

"I have no idea," I say in all honesty. "It's late and most restaurants will have taken the last food orders by now." Then an idea hits me, and although it might seem like the worst place for a date, I'm really craving a bowl of chili. "Actually, I do know a place. But it's nothing fancy and we'll have to take the subway."

"Hey, I don't care about fancy." Zelda spreads her arms, gesturing to our simple surroundings. "I've shown you my world, now show me yours."

16

_____

"This is where I grew up," I say as we enter the diner. I've enjoyed holding Zelda's hand during the walk from the subway and I love how she opens the door for me. If this is a date, she's doing a great job as I'm not just comfortable and relaxed in her company, but also enormously turned on, knowing there's more to come. We take a seat at 'my' booth by the window opposite the counter, from where my mother used to keep an eye on me while serving customers.

It's an old-fashioned diner in the most traditional sense and the interior has not changed since I was a kid. The long bar with worn-out red stools, the matching red booths, the black and white checkered floor tiles, the photographs of the owner and her family on the walls, alongside framed reviews—now faded and worn—from when this place was still in its heyday. Even the napkin holders and salt and pepper pots are still the same; a hideous shade of eighties lilac. The lighting is unforgiving and the smell of stale coffee hangs in the air like poison, yet this place feels like a part of me.

"Where you grew up? Is this where your mom works?" Zelda asks.

"It sure is. This is the diner my mom's worked at for the past twenty-five years. She used to put me right here at this table when she was struggling to find a sitter for me." I smile at the memory as I look out of the window. The one thing that's changed is the view, but fortunately for the better. Instead of the old warehouse that used to be opposite the diner, the road is now lined with beautiful redbrick buildings that house quirky shops and a cute ice cream parlor.

"So, you spent a lot of time here?"

"Yes. Some people may find that a sad thought, but I liked coming here. The other waitresses fussed over me non-stop, and I had my school work to do, plus they gave me milk and cookies, so I was happy."

"Is your mom here now?" Zelda asks. If she's worried about meeting her, she's not letting it show.

"No, she's off tonight," I say with a chuckle. "Otherwise I wouldn't have brought you here." Spotting a couple of familiar faces, I see that one of the regulars—a guy whose name I never learned—is still having his late-night black coffee and scrambled eggs, and another woman who looks familiar is talking to Marjorie, the owner. "I still come here regularly. It's just easier to meet my mom here than at her apartment, and she always keeps a plate aside for me if I give her a head's up. It's not exactly the fanciest place in the world, but they do a great chili."

As if on cue, Marjorie narrows her eyes at me from the counter, her dimples just as deep as when I first met her many years ago. Seeing her warm smile widen always makes me smile too. "Lucy?"

"That's the lady of the house," I whisper, and give

Marjorie a wave. "Yes, it's me. It's good to see you again. How are you?"

"I'm good, honey," Marjorie says, rushing to our table. "What about you? My God, you look so pretty tonight. How's life at Bergman's?"

"It's going good, thanks." I get up to give her a hug and chuckle at her question. Marjorie never crosses the river and thinks working at Bergman's is the height of sophistication. Even though she knows I'm studying to become a lawyer, she keeps encouraging me to apply for a full-time job there instead. "And you're looking great, too."

"Oh, I don't know about that." Marjorie chuckles and tousles my hair, just like she used to do when I was little. "Does your mom know you're here? She'll be back from her break any minute, but I can give her a shout if you—"

"Mom's here?" I interrupt her. Realizing I'm in trouble, I scan the diner for the nearest exit and try to come up with an excuse to leave. Even if we sneak out now, Marjorie will tell my mother I was here, and she'll never forgive me for not saying hello. I don't want her to see me with Zelda though, as she'll just make assumptions. I've never introduced a girlfriend to my mother; I've never gotten serious enough with someone for that. No doubt she'll think this is a big deal, especially if she notices our undeniable chemistry which is only growing as the night progresses.

I flinch as I see my mom coming out of the break room where she usually works her way through a black coffee and a pile of French fries after smoking a cigarette outside. She spots me and comes over to our table with a baffled expression on her face. "Lucy, my love. What are you doing here?"

"Hey, Mom. I was hungry," I say with a shrug.

"Why didn't you message me to let me know you were coming? I could have planned my break around your visit."

I give her a hug and a big kiss on her cheek. She looks good this evening. Her dark hair is neatly pinned up, she's wearing makeup, which is unusual for her, and I see she's had her nails done too. "I thought you were off tonight." Rubbing her arm, I sit back down and hope for the best.

"So, you only want to come in on my days off?" My mother steps back, props her hands on her hips and frowns. "Are you avoiding me or something?"

"No, it's not like that, it's..." I shake my head. "Never mind."

"Well, as you can see, I'm here. Everyone wants time off for the holidays, so I offered to work overtime," she continues, casting a curious glance at Zelda. I know I won't hear the end of this, but since I have company, she's letting me off the hook for now. "Just like you, honey." Then she turns to Zelda. "And who have we here?"

Zelda doesn't seem startled at all and gives my mother a warm smile. "Hi. I'm Zelda."

"Zelda? And you're..." My mother smiles back as she narrows her eyes at Zelda, and I know it won't take much for her to figure out that she's gay. Her androgynous looks, the way she carries herself with that butch confidence and her arm behind me, resting on the back of the bench kind of give her away. "On a date with my daughter?"

"No," I say before Zelda has the chance to answer. "We just came here for a quick bite to eat. Zelda works at Bergman's. We're colleagues." It's not entirely true but it will do for now.

"Aha." Going by my mother's expression, she doesn't believe me, but she doesn't pry either. "Well, it's nice to finally meet one of Lucy's friends."

Marjorie, who's disappeared for a moment, has returned with a basket of fresh garlic bread and a jug of juice. The

85

latter amuses me as I'm not a kid anymore, but I gladly accept it and pour us both a glass. "Dinner's on me," she says, rubbing my shoulder. "Let me guess. Chili?"

17

_____

"Your mom seems lovely." Zelda puts her arm around me as we exit the subway station and head to her apartment. The winter air is dry and crisp, and the city seems so alive tonight that I'm enjoying the casual stroll. "And that chili was awesome. I think I've found my new favorite place to eat."

"I'm glad you enjoyed it." I let Zelda pull me in closer and inhale deeply, taking in her scent. "Sorry about my mom though; I didn't plan on introducing her to you."

"I figured that from your reaction," Zelda says with a chuckle. "You looked like you were about to run off when she appeared, but it's not like she knows we're sleeping together."

"Trust me; my mom knows everything. I think she might be psychic," I joke.

"And would it be so bad if she knew we were on a date?" Zelda asks.

I shrug. "Not necessarily. But I don't want her to think you're my girlfriend."

A subtle expression of pain passes over Zelda's soft

features, but she nods in agreement. "Right. I get that." She slides her hand down to my behind and rests it there. "Are you spending the holidays with her?"

"No. Mom is working, and I have to study. But it's not a big deal; I'm not into Christmas, never have been." I love the feel of Zelda's hand possessively pressing against my behind. My mind wanders off again and I feel a familiar yearning as I remember this afternoon in the utility room. It's the sexiest encounter I've ever had, and I know it will never leave my memory.

"Really? You don't like Christmas?" Zelda sounds surprised.

"No, not my thing," I say, and try to focus on the conversation instead of the sensual flashbacks. Her hand on my ass is certainly not helping. "To me, Christmas is just a commercialized marketing stunt. I don't get the forced fun and the obligatory gatherings, and Christmas carols drive me nuts. Seriously, they're like an assault to my ears," I say, rolling my eyes as a stirring chorus of '*Joy to the World*' blasts through an open window. "In my opinion, the month of December brings out the worst in people. I literally see customers fighting over products during their last-minute shopping sprees at Bergman's and the ones that shop through the personal shopping team are just trying to assuage their guilt for neglecting their family and friends over the year. Besides that, I think Christmas is nonsense on every level. It's not like anyone really knows when Jesus was born."

Zelda laughs and shoots me an amused look. "You really do have a strong opinion on Christmas."

"I do." I slip my hand into her back pocket, smiling as I feel her muscles tense. "What about you?"

"I'm not sure if I feel brave enough to say this in your presence, but I kind of like Christmas," Zelda admits.

"Although my parents never took part in the commercial aspect of the holidays, I have good memories. My mother used to play guitar on Christmas Eve while my father, my brother and I sang carols together. We cooked nice food, went for long walks in the snow, and I remember the abundance of candles like it was yesterday. My mom has a thing for them." She pauses. "But it's not just the memories, I like this time of year. Burning candles—I have a thing for them too—and lighting a fire when it's cold outside, the smell of pine from the Christmas trees and walking around the city at night looking at the festive window displays and the lights that are twinkling... Everything just looks and feels so magical... Also, I like the seasonal specialized coffees they have on offer in December," she says jokingly, pointing at a Starbucks we're passing.

"Fair enough. I like those too." I look around and realize that she's right about the lights. The city does look beautiful tonight. The buildings on restaurant row in Hell's Kitchen are covered in string lights and I can see the Christmas trees and lavish decorations though their big windows. They serve food from all over the world here and even though everything is closed now, the smell of exotic spices still hangs in the air. I like this neighborhood, and it suits her.

"Fuck. You have no idea how much I want you," Zelda says out of nowhere with a look that could set fire to ice.

"I think I have an idea," I whisper, meeting her hungry eyes. "I don't know how it's possible, but I want you all the time."

Zelda nods slowly in agreement, then asks: "Do you like to be spanked?"

My breath hitches and I take a moment to process her unexpected question. Normally, my answer to that would be 'no' but truthfully, I've never tried it with another partner and the idea of her hand slamming down on my behind is suddenly surprisingly appealing. "I don't know."

Again, she nods, and her intense stare is driving me wild. "Would you like to find out?"

"Yes," I hear myself say. My panties are soaked at the thought of surrendering to her and I can tell from Zelda's reaction that my answer has aroused her too. What follows is an intense sexual silence—the quiet sound of longing and anticipation—and by the time we get to her blue door I can hardly contain myself as I wait for her to unlock it.

18

———

"Welcome back." Zelda switches on the lights, dims them, then goes to work with lighting the many candles while I remove my trench coat and my scarf.

"I love your studio," I say, imagining myself living in a place like this. I know this is no time for small talk, but as I'm nervous following our brief conversation and have no idea what I'm getting myself into, I want her to make the first move.

"Thank you, I like it too." Zelda walks over to the kitchenette, holds up a bottle of wine and when I shake my head, a smile plays around her mouth as she puts it back in the rack. It's clear that she was just being polite; we both know what we want and it's not wine. "I bought it last year. It's a good feeling to own my own place; it's not something I ever thought I'd accomplish, especially not in New York." She inches closer, her burning blue eyes making me melt on the spot as she stares at me. "But let's park the real estate talk for later, shall we?"

"Sure," I whisper, shivering when she cups my neck and kisses me softly. Our kiss soon turns heated as I slide off her coat and lift her sweater to find the warm skin that I've been longing to feel under my fingertips. She moans softly and I push myself tighter against her when her hands move under my blouse. I've missed her hands. They take what they want and bring me immense pleasure in the process. My thumb brushes over her nipples through the fabric of her sports bra, drawing a louder moan from her, and I feel her shudder against me before she shifts her thigh between my legs. I'm throbbing, and the pressure feels so amazing that I let out a frustrated sigh when she breaks the kiss and moves back, just a little.

For a while, she just stands there and watches me, like she's trying to figure out a game plan. "So, Lucy..." She pauses. "Last time you were here, you said you'd been good..." She arches a brow, her breath heavy against mine now. Kissing me has turned her on more than I realized, and I'm feeling a sense of impatience that is bordering on desperation.

"Mm-hmm." I love Zelda's games and that she's full of surprises. Her whole demeanor has changed, and her acting is convincing to the point that it almost scares me. Gone is her amazing smile and carefree attitude. Instead, an intriguing seriousness takes over her features as her full brows pull together over now cold eyes.

"Have you been good since?" The flash of anticipation I see in her eyes is ever so subtle, but I know exactly what answer she's expecting.

"I'm not sure," I say, playing along. "I may have done something naughty."

"Oh yeah?" Zelda's eyes darken, and she takes a firm hold of me with one arm, wrapping it around my waist while the other lowers to my ass and squeezes it hard. She likes my answer. "What did you do that was so bad?"

I'm quiet for a beat, still deciding whether I really want this. "I let Santa fuck me in the utility room at work." The words leave my lips in a breathless whisper and I moan when she runs her tongue over the side of my neck.

"Did you now?" she whispers in my ear. "That was very, very naughty indeed." Pulling away to look at me, Zelda licks her lips. "And did you like being fucked by Santa?"

"Yes." I stare right back at her, letting her know I'm fully on board now. I'm excited by her domineering tone and the fact that I have no idea what she will do to me. "I loved it."

"You loved it, huh? Then I hope it was worth the punishment that you're about to receive." She takes a wide stance and crosses her arms in front of her chest. "Turn around, Lucy." I'm still processing the order and when I don't immediately comply, she does it for me. "I said, turn around." Her tone is suddenly harsh and cold, and so is the surface against my thighs when she spins me around, lifts up my skirt and pushes me against the refrigerator.

Grabbing my wrists, I feel her strength as she brings them behind my back and holds them there with one hand. Her breath is heavy in my ear as she leans in and whispers: "Would you like to find out what Santa does to naughty girls?"

Everything about this passive position has me so turned on that I have trouble speaking, and I can feel the heavy throb of my pulse pounding at the base of my neck as well as between my legs. "Yes."

"What was that? I can't hear you."

"Yes," I say, louder this time. I find myself shifting from one high-heeled foot to the other, amazed as to how wet she's made me.

"Okay." There's a long silence and my mind goes crazy with anticipation as I wait. "Tell me if you want me to stop," she says then, her voice a little softer this time so I know this is not part of the roleplay. "Stop is good enough." Without warning, her hand lands firmly on my behind and I jump and gasp at the sting it leaves.

I'm baffled by how much I like it. There's no time to analyze my reaction any further though, as she spanks me again in the same spot. I feel my cheek glowing and I'm very aware that my tiny panties aren't covering much at all.

"Stop?" she asks.

I swallow hard and close my eyes as I shake my head against the refrigerator, "No."

As soon as I've replied, Zelda raises her hand and slaps my other cheek, harder and twice in quick concession, then squeezes it so firmly that I flinch.

"Fuck, I love your ass." She stops and stands still behind me. Even though I can't see her, I can feel her smile. "I think you like this, Lucy..."

She's right; my legs are trembling and my whole body feels alive from this new sensation. "I do," I admit in a thin voice.

"Good." Zelda lets go of my wrists, tears open my blouse and cups my breasts, pulling me back against her. Massaging them with her skilled hands, she lulls me into a false sense of security, letting me believe the spanking is over. I'm not sure whether I'm relieved or disappointed; the rush of adrenaline I felt got me hooked and I think I want her to do it again. Inhaling deeply against my hair, she lets out a quiet moan and slips her fingers under the edge of my bra, then pinches my nipples until I gasp—teetering on the edge of pleasure and pain. "Then I will give you more. Stay there and don't look."

After Zelda steps away from me, I hear her rummage through the kitchen drawer and pull something out. I can't see what it is as I'm facing the other way, and I'm not sure I want to know. She takes me by the hand and walks me to the kitchen island. "Bend over and place your hands on the counter." Her tone is flat, almost businesslike, as if she's wrapping up a meeting. It's hot, so hot that a part of me wants to turn around and kiss her.

"Just tell me to stop and I will," she says, stroking my stinging behind. She wedges her fingers under the edge of my panties and moves her hand between my legs. "Mmm... you are so ready for this." When she skims my sensitive lips, I push back, desperate for contact.

"What did I tell you?" Immediately Zelda pulls her hand away. "Don't move or there will be consequences."

It's hard to believe that I like her talking to me in this domineering way. I would normally scold anyone who had the audacity to speak to me like this, but I find myself settling into the role of a submissive like I've been craving this my whole life. Have I been craving this?

Slowly, she peels off my panties and pulls them down. The drenched fabric is skimming my ankles and I'm almost embarrassed at how visibly aroused I am as I step out of them. She hikes my skirt up farther and I feel vulnerable, knowing that she is looking at me. My fear of the unknown sends a sizzle of desire up my spine and deep into my core while I wait. And wait. And wait.

When I least expect it, something hard lands on my behind again. Closing my eyes tight, I clench my jaw and groan as it hits me three times. Whatever she is spanking me with has way more impact than her hand. The surface is different; much smaller and denser, concentrating the pain in one area, and I suspect it's a silicon cooking utensil of some description. She swats my other cheek, lower, almost hitting the inside of my thigh, and this time I cry out as it really hurts. The pain only lasts for a beat though. As she squeezes and caresses the spot, the sting is replaced by a tingling in my super-responsive nerve endings, culminating in a throbbing sensation between my legs. I didn't know my ass was an erogenous zone, and I didn't know I liked to surrender, but her actions really do it for me.

The feeling it stirs in me is one of freedom—sexual freedom—something that is entirely new to me. I feel desired, and curiously powerful. I'm the center of her world right now; she's here for me and I can make her stop at any moment, taking away our joint pleasure.

She strikes me again and I groan in both agony and pleasure. "Stop?" she asks.

"No." I'm so on edge that I'm hoping any kind of contact, even pain, will give me some release.

"Very well. Spread your legs." Zelda taps the inside of my thigh with whatever she's been spanking me with. "Do you really want this?" she asks. "I need to hear you say it."

"Yes. Just do it," I say through ragged breaths. "I want this." Once more, I wait and wait, and nothing happens. My heart is beating in my throat and I'm stretched so taut that my stomach muscles feel sore. It's the not knowing that makes me apprehensive and when the object lands between my legs and swats my pussy from behind, I let out a loud curse. "Fuck!" The pain makes my clit spasm in the most delicious way and I have trouble standing still.

"You like that," she says again before she gets down on her knees behind me and grabs me by my hips. Burying her face between my legs, she runs her tongue over me, skimming my clit and inching inside me until I scream out my release, climaxing with a force that makes me delirious. For long moments, I can't think, see, or hear. I can only feel, and when the intensity of my orgasm ebbs away, I lose all strength and sink to the floor in a post-orgasmic heap.

Zelda catches me and holds me in her arms while she leans back against the kitchen island. "Are you okay?"

I nod, unable to get a word out. My chest is heaving in her strong grip, and my eyes flutter closed as she strokes my hair. "That was fucking amazing," I whisper, breathing heavily.

She chuckles and kisses my cheek, then rests her temple against mine. "You, my Lucy, are very, very good at being naughty."

19

"What time is it?" I ask in a sleepy voice. I've dozed off in Zelda's arms, engulfed in the warmth of her body. My previous lovers don't compare to her sexually, and I'm tired and spent, more relaxed than I've been in a very long time. When I'm with her, nothing else matters, and my thoughts haven't drifted to studying once.

Zelda turns her head to check her phone sitting on her nightstand. "One a.m.," she mumbles, pulling me closer.

"Fuck. I've got to go." I don't understand how I've been here for hours—time seems to fly when I'm with Zelda—but I do know that I have an early shift this morning and staying over is a bad idea.

"You don't have to," she protests, blinking against the light when I switch on a lamp.

"Sorry," I whisper and quickly slip into my clothes, stuffing my lingerie into my purse. It's not just the early shift. I've never spent the night with a lover, and I suddenly feel restless and my need to get out of here kicks in, but Zelda doesn't need to know that. "I'll see you at work?"

There's no answer as Zelda has already fallen asleep

again. She looks so sweet, curled up on her side, tangled in the covers that I'm almost tempted to stay. Her hair is messy, and the pillow she is wrapped around has left an imprint on her cheek—a pattern of creases now marring one side of her boyishly handsome face. It strikes me again how incredibly attractive she is, and I allow myself to indulge in the sight of her for a little longer before I leave quietly and hail a cab to take me back to campus.

As we drive through the night, I watch the world go by and marvel at how pretty New York is. The Christmas decorations have brought the city to life in a way I've never noticed before. I suppose having a crush makes me see everything through rose-colored glasses but I'm now thinking that perhaps I've been too harsh with my criticism with regards to Christmas. Just because I've never celebrated Christmas doesn't mean I can't embrace it just a little. For the first time in my life, I feel a hint of excitement about the approaching holidays and wonder if my mother will finish work earlier so I can stop by her house with some food and a bottle of wine because if anyone deserves it, it's her.

Already, I miss the closeness of Zelda's body and although my heart longs to go back to the safety of her arms, my head is telling me that I really need to start focusing on what's important again. She's been a huge distraction and my to-do list has been neglected. I'd planned to use the quiet time on campus to my advantage but that hasn't happened. Never mind. I only have a few more long days at Bergman's as we close early on Christmas Eve. As soon as I leave the building, I'll concentrate on my studies and internship applications.

The thought of not seeing Zelda at work after that makes me a little sad because I've really enjoyed this week with her. Sex has never been high on my priority list but now I seem to have a one-track mind. Shivers run through me as I think of her dominant tone, the explosive pleasure she gave me and the tender lovemaking afterwards... I can still taste her on my lips, and as I lick them and recall her moans as I made her come with my tongue, I clench my thighs together.

But it wasn't just the sex. I've enjoyed getting to know her, and I've even opened up to her. Hell, she even met my mother, I think with a silent chuckle.

"NYU campus?" the driver asks, even though I've already told him where to drop me.

"Yeah." I smile back at him as our eyes meet in the rearview mirror.

"Okay. I was just checking. It must be quiet there right now. With everyone going home to see their families..." He clears his throat. "You going home for the holidays? Or are you staying there?" His voice trails off at the word 'there' and if his expression is anything to go by, he thinks staying on campus is the equivalent of being in hell this time of year.

"No, I'm not going home. I have to study, and my mother is working. But that's okay," I quickly add. This is my choice and his pity is the last thing I need. "What about you? Any plans?"

"I'm taking Christmas Day off," he says, his smile widening. "My son and his family are flying in from Washington. We haven't seen them in a while so my wife and I are looking forward to having some time with the grandkids."

"That sounds like fun."

"Yeah. We love seeing the kids get excited over presents and my wife's a great cook." Again, he regards me through the rearview mirror, as if he can't quite work me out. A young woman by herself over Christmas on a near-empty campus. I bet he feels sorry for me. "Are you at least having some nice food? Visiting your ma after work?"

"Sure," I say, hoping to be let off the hook. I know he means well, but I hate this pressure. "I'll go see her." There's only one thing I find more annoying than listening to Christmas carols, and that's people who don't understand that I simply don't care. They feel the need to get to the bottom of the whys and the wherefores, puzzled beyond belief, as not celebrating Christmas just isn't an option in their world.

"Good. That makes me feel better."

I suppress an eye roll and wisely keep quiet until he pulls up at the campus gates. "Well, enjoy spending time with your family," I say, handing him the cash. "Keep the change."

"Thank you. Merry Christmas."

I manage a smile before I close the door and give him a wave. "Merry Christmas."

20

As Christmas is fast approaching, the staff at Bergman's are cheerful and full of energy. Our customers on the other hand, are stressed and grumpy as some of our most popular items are sold out. I let out a sigh of relief when I slip into the break room, happy to escape the panicked mothers who are fighting over toys and video games.

"Hey, you." I walk up to Zelda when I see her sipping a coffee while reading through a file at a table.

"Hey, Lucy." Her face lights up as she pulls down her beard and shoots me a big smile before her eyes lower to my legs. "You look good. Really good."

"Thank you," I say as a blush creeps up my cheeks. I've put more effort in than I normally would this morning; my red lips are accentuated with gloss and my hair is straightened and shiny. I make myself a coffee and take a seat next to her. "What are you doing?"

"Just reading some instructions on the drop-off round. I'm starting tomorrow after Bergman's closes." She subtly places a hand on my thigh under the table, and I giggle as I slap it away, scanning the room for onlookers. There's a handful of people gathered around the coffee machine but they're all animatedly talking about their Christmas plans. "Want to come for a walk with me after work?" She winks. "Unless you've had enough of me. I don't want to be presumptuous, but I've really enjoyed our time together and although you took off in the early hours, I have a feeling you like spending time with me too.

"Oh yes, about that..." I bite my lip and pause. "Sorry I left so abruptly, but I needed fresh clothes and—"

"Hey, it's okay. I didn't mean it like that." Zelda lowers her voice. "We've only just met; no pressure whatsoever. I just think you're sexy and cute and fun, that's all."

"I like you too." My stomach flutters physically at her words, and as soon as her soft blue eyes meet mine, I feel my resolve crumbling. Who am I kidding? Of course I want to go for a walk with her. Right now, I'd do anything as long as I get to spend more time with her. "Where do you want to go?"

"Central Park is beautiful at Christmas time."

I throw my head back and laugh. "Are you trying to get me to enter into the Christmas spirit? Because that's not going to work with me."

"We'll see about that." Zelda winks, then turns back to her paperwork and flips to the next page. "What the fuck?" her face pulls into a grimace.

"What's wrong?" She looks so shocked that I want to rip the page out of her hand and read it.

"You'll never believe who will be doing the Christmas rounds with me."

"Who?" I lean in to take a look and can't help but laugh when I read the name of 'Santa's helper'. It looks like Bergman's has employed twelve other Santas and they've all been assigned an elf. "Andy? Andy the Elf? Oh my God... Are you sure that's the right Andy?" My eyes widen when Zelda nods, her shoulders dropping in defeat.

"Yeah, I recognize his surname," she says, holding up the file. "Our talent agency sent the vacancy out to everyone so it makes sense." She groans. "Two days with that scumbag... I'd quit now if it wasn't for all those kids who are eagerly waiting for Santa to visit."

"Could someone else step in as Santa for you?"

Zelda shakes her head. "I doubt they'll be able to find a replacement for me on such short notice."

"Right..." A mad idea starts forming in my head, then. An idea we could all benefit from, including Andy. "Is Andy in today?" I ask.

"Yeah. I've seen him. He was enquiring about our arrangement, and I told him to fuck off. Why?"

"Oh, nothing, just wondering if he's reported us to HR," I lie. "But as I haven't been called into their office yet, I suppose he hasn't. I get up again, take a long drink of my coffee and pour the rest down the sink. "I'll see you after work, then?"

Before Zelda has the chance to answer, I rush down the corridor and I'm relieved to see Andy is just heading into the utility room. I can hardly believe what I'm about to propose; perhaps this crush is making me foolish because all I can think of is that I want to be near her.

"Andy..." I give him my brightest smile as he turns, but he stops me when I'm about to follow him in.

"You have no jurisdiction here, Lucy," he says as if the utility room is a crime scene.

"Of course. I apologize." I resist rolling my eyes and step back into the corridor while I hold open the door. "I was wondering if I could talk to you about something..."

"Have you spoken to management regarding my nomination for Employee of the Month?"

"No. That's not going to happen. I don't appreciate being blackmailed, but I do have another proposal that might make you happy." He doesn't deserve my help in any way, but I'm doing this for entirely selfish reasons, so I guess that makes it okay.

Although he's playing it cool, I can tell Andy is all ears—appropriate for an elf. Deep down he must have known he'd gone too far and that his behavior was unacceptable. I see his expression soften a little. Perhaps it's surprise at my willingness to do something for him after the stunt he pulled. "Shoot," he says, glancing at his watch.

"Have you heard who you've been paired with for the personalized deliveries yet?"

Andy looks confused. "No... Wait, how do you know I signed up for that?"

"Zelda told me. You'll be doing the rounds with her." I try not to laugh at his baffled expression.

"No..."

"Yep. You two will be spending lots of time together." I pause for effect. "But, lucky for you, I can help you out."

21

I've borrowed Bridget's sneakers and I'm glad I wore my warmest coat to work this morning; a black woolen trench coat with a thick, matching scarf and a faux-fur black hat. Zelda has changed into jeans, a thick sweater, snow boots and a puffer jacket, and she looks super cute with her gray marl beanie.

"You should have kept your Santa costume on," I joke as we exit Bergman's and walk into the madness that is New York at Christmas. 34th Street is tinsel town and my eyes hurt each time I leave the building. Baubles the size of trucks line the street and the window displays of the department stores here give Disney World a run for its money.

"Are we doing the whole Christmas tour?" I ask.

"Of course." Zelda chuckles. "When was the last time you saw the tree at the Rockefeller Center?"

"I've actually never seen it," I admit. "I tend to avoid it and I usually go straight home after work."

Zelda's eyes widen as she gasps. "What? You've never skated at The Rink in front of the tree and under the iconic golden statue of Prometheus? What about Times Square?"

She gawks at me in disbelief when I shake my head. "Okay, Lucy. We're going to change that right now. A Christmas walk through Midtown Manhattan might be your idea of hell, but I promise you it's going to be fun." She takes my gloved hand. "Are you ready?"

"Do I have a choice?"

"No."

I smile at her and shrug. "Then let's do it."

Walking with Zelda is anything but hell. In fact, I'm loving the feel of her hand in mine and our closeness each time she pulls me in to place a kiss on my cheek. When I find myself staring at her in adoration, I realize I'm fucked. I'm falling for her hard and there's nothing I can do to stop it.

I've never had a crush this bad and I've come to the conclusion that giving into it is much easier than fighting it. By now, I've run out of excuses why I should. Sure, my career is important to me. But this feels good, not to mention being with her is addictive. The hit of happiness and zest for life I get from her is giving me so much energy that it feels like I'm floating through the streets and admittedly, I'm even appreciating the Christmas atmosphere tonight.

Time Square is even crazier, with huge projections of angels and Santa Claus flashing over the skyscrapers. Midtown Manhattan is lit up like nowhere else in the world and I suspect it runs on enough energy to power a small country. It's cold now, with the temperatures in New York plummeting below zero at night, and I wrap my scarf tighter around my neck before hooking my arm through Zelda's.

"You're right, this is fun," I admit. "Wild, but fun."

"See? I've converted you already." She smiles at me and cheers when a Spanish guitarist finishes a rendition of '*Feliz Navidad*', then throws a dollar bill into his case. He's not the only one performing; carol-singing buskers stand on every corner, wrapped in big coats while they belt out classics, encouraging passersby to join in.

Zelda is chivalrous and sweet, and I love how she gets excited by the decorations and sings along to the street musicians. Everywhere is crammed with tourists, of course, but that's something I'm used to in New York and it doesn't bother me. In fact, seeing how excited a group of German tourists are as they stare in wonder at the festive displays, makes me feel proud to be a New Yorker.

We pass food carts that offer roasted chestnuts, apple cider, hot chocolate, spiced cookies and of course New York's iconic hot dogs. All around us people are trying to sell silly electronic Christmas toys, Santa hats and stuffed animals.

I laugh when Zelda buys me a hideous looking elf statue with laser beam eyes that flash to the beat of the house music blasting through his big ears when she presses his belly. "Thanks. That must be the most romantic present anyone had ever given me."

Zelda laughs too. "Well, I wanted to give you something to remember me by. I'll be doing the rounds over the next few days and you said you had to study and that your career comes first so I don't expect us to see much of each other after the holidays." She smiles, letting me know it's no big deal. "But this way, you'll remember our time in the utility room and think of me each time this little monster's eyes light up."

I should be amused but her words make me sad. If I've given her the impression this is the end, then she's wrong, because I don't want this to end. I haven't yet told her I'll be joining her tomorrow and I'm already looking forward to seeing the look on her face when I turn up. "Well, I hope we can still meet up every now and then."

Zelda arches a brow and her smile widens. "Really?"

"Yeah. Just, you know, for some fun."

"You mean for sex?" She licks her lips and pulls me in, then kisses me. "Because I'm down for that."

We've reached the Rockefeller Center and I'm really starting to get sucked into the festivities. Zelda's enthusiasm is rubbing off on me, making me want to join in.

"Now, you need to immerse yourself because this is important." Zelda and I stare up at the enormous tree—our next stop on the walk. "As a New Yorker, it's a crime that you've never seen the Rockefeller Center Christmas tree in its full glory before, so you'd better appreciate it."

"It's impressive," I agree. The famous tree is decorated with multicolored lights and is topped with a huge illuminated star. In front of it, the ice rink is filled with people skating, taking pictures or enjoying a hot drink from the sidelines.

A choir is singing Christmas carols in front of the tree, and for the first time, hearing the familiar songs doesn't annoy me. Their harmonies are perfectly on point and their timbre truly touching as '*Gloria in Excelsis*' rings through the air. I lean into Zelda and rest my head on her shoulder, genuinely enjoying the concert.

Once the angelic voices have subsided, we continue our walk and stop off for a takeout hot chocolate with marshmallows, gossiping about the staff at Bergman's. Zelda shares funny anecdotes of her time there and being an actress, she's a really good storyteller; the toddler who pulled down her beard, the little girl who figured out Santa had boobies, and the mother who flirted with her, then found out Zelda was a woman and ran off in a panic. Her lips taste of chocolate now and I simply can't stop kissing her. I feel like I'm sixteen all over again, out on the town with my first girlfriend.

Just before we reach Central Park it starts to snow, and the excitement is visible in the crowd. Murmurs grow louder as people look skyward, gazing at the white flakes against the black night. I'm amazed at how perfect the timing is. For someone who doesn't like Christmas, this night couldn't have been more enchanting and the snow is just the icing on the cake.

"God, you look beautiful tonight." Zelda brushes away a flake from my nose and kisses my forehead, then cups my face and looks at me like I'm the only person who matters to her.

"Thank you," I whisper, equally captivated by her handsome frost-kissed face that I just can't seem to get enough of. I could look at her forever and never get bored. I'm not sure what we're doing but I know one thing; people who are on a second date do not behave like this. They can't possibly be this comfortable and relaxed around each other, and I doubt this dynamic is normal either. It's explosive to say the least and every time our eyes meet the desire is mutual. "Do you like snow?" I ask, pulling my hat further over my head.

"Of course I like snow. I'm Santa." Zelda shoots me a smile. "It makes the whole world look prettier. And quieter," she adds. "Have you ever gone for an early morning walk in the snow?"

"Yes, I love it," I say. "It's so peaceful. Especially in New York, it's like the snow dampens the city noise." Inhaling deeply, I take her hand and allow myself to be swept away by the Christmas charm of Central Park as it starts snowing harder, suddenly covering our surroundings in a fragile layer of white. The carriage house we're passing looks cozy with its traditional decorations and food stands upfront. Carriage rides are popular with tourists and wedding parties over Christmas, but I've never seen the carriages look as spectacular as they do tonight. They're decorated with tinsel, tiny string lights and pine branches, and are pulled by beautifully groomed horses and filled with happy people.

Trees and park benches catch the snowflakes, changing the landscape around us, and the blanket of white, powdery beauty settles like a soft cushion underneath our feet. It's busy here tonight, yet it feels like we're the only two people in the world.

We stroll past Wollman Rink and soon we're surrounded by skyscrapers and string light covered trees that make me feel like I'm walking in a light box. I have no idea how long we've wandered through this wonderland when Zelda stops and looks at me regretfully.

"I'm sorry, but I have to go and surprise my niece and nephew soon. I wanted to use the Santa suit to my advantage while I have it, so I promised my brother I'd swing by tonight as I'll be working over Christmas."

"That's sweet of you. You didn't tell me your brother had kids. How old are they?"

"Four and six. They're so cute; Marty and Mira. It's past their bedtime but they're off school and a surprise visit from Santa is extra fun late at night. I have a little present for each of them and my brother will give me some presents from him and his wife to put under the tree."

"I bet they'll be super excited."

"Yeah." Zelda's smile is warm and sweet as she talks about them and I love everything I'm learning about her. "I adore those little troublemakers; I just hope they won't recognize me."

"Just put on that funny old man's voice of yours and you'll be fine," I say, taking both her hands. I realize I must look like I'm smitten with her and truth be told, I am. The need to touch her and be near her is strong, so strong that I jump at any opportunity for physical contact. "Where's your costume?"

"It's at Bergman's. The security guard on duty tonight gave me his number and promised to bring my bag to the back door, so I'll go and pick it up first."

"Okay. I'll take the subway home, then." Glancing at my watch, I note it's almost nine p.m. The hours have flown by and I've truly enjoyed our walk. It's been romantic, sexy, fun, magical and everything in between. Zelda seems genuinely interested in my career plans and she told me about her life working in musicals. We've laughed, talked, eaten food from the street carts, made out at every opportunity and walked for miles. Our night may almost be over but the white dreamscape will extend beyond Central Park, allowing me to hold onto this magical feeling for just a little longer.

"So, did I manage to change your mind about Christmas?" she asks as we head for the exit.

"Maybe a little," I say, not quite ready to admit defeat. "When people used to refer to getting in the Christmas spirit, I didn't understand what they meant by that, but I think I get it now. The city is wonderful tonight, and your company has been perfect."

"Good. I've really enjoyed it too." She kisses my temple and pulls me in as we cross the road. "But it's probably a good thing I have to go; I'm aware that I've been distracting you way too much lately."

"I've loved every minute of you distracting me, but I'm

sure you've got things you need to get on with too, like preparing for your rehearsals. And yes, it's about time I finally get to those internship applications I was supposed to send out."

"The letters you told me about?"

"Yeah."

A hint of regret flashes across Zelda's features as she lingers at the subway entrance. "The other night, when I made that comment about divorce lawyers... I didn't mean to offend you."

"You didn't. It's fine."

"No, it's not fine. I made fun of you, but I need you to know that I really admire you for your drive. I don't know many people who know exactly what they want to do with their life and stick to their plan, and I get that your career comes first. But then again..." She shrugs and her wide smile is back. "It's almost Christmas, and it feels like that time of year when we deserve a break, doesn't it?"

"You're right. I rarely do something like this, just for fun." Meeting her eyes, I lean in and kiss her for what feels like the millionth time. "So, thank you for tonight."

"You're most welcome." Zelda straightens herself and steps away, then changes her mind and pulls me in for another kiss. "Sorry, I can't seem to get enough of those lips." She chuckles. "I'll see you at work tomorrow? Christmas Eve... Santa might even have a present for you if you're lucky."

"I thought Santa didn't give out presents to girls on his naughty list," I joke.

Zelda's eyebrow shoots up and she licks her lips. "Are you kidding me?" She winks. "Santa loves naughty girls."

22

I have trouble sleeping and can't seem to think of anything else but Zelda. She's occupying my mind with sexual fantasies and although I love to indulge in them, it's not helping me on the studying front. Concentrating has been hard and after four hours of staring at my application letters—only making insignificant changes that won't make a difference whatsoever—I undress and crawl into bed.

I'm grateful Shelley has gone back home, or at least I assume she has, as she's not here and her bed is made. It's weird how I always look forward to having the room to myself, yet I miss her when she's away.

Reaching for my phone to check the time, I decide to message Zelda. It's late but I have a feeling she's a night owl and if she's sleeping then I'll apologize. *'Hey. It's Lucy. How was your surprise visit?'* It's strange to type the sentence as it's the first thing I've ever sent to her. She only gave me her number tonight and having it in my phone has been testing my willpower for hours. Almost immediately, a reply comes in.

'Hey, Lucy. Yes, it was fun! They didn't recognize me and it

was so unexpected that poor Mira almost fainted with happiness. What are you doing?'

I reply with a laughing emoji, then send another message. *'I'm in bed. Trouble sleeping.'* Finally, I add, *'Sorry if I woke you.'*

'You didn't.'

A minute passes and I'm about to put my phone away as it felt like she was ending the conversation, when another message comes in.

'What are you wearing?'

I squeeze my thighs together at her message and bite my lip as I type a reply. *'Nothing.'*

'Mmm... Naked in your dorm room? I like that. It's my ultimate fantasy.'

I giggle and take my time to think of a reply. Failing to come up with something witty on the spot, I decide instead to go with something bold. *'My roommate is away. NYU Greenwich Village, 2B028.'*

'Don't tempt me.'

I smile at that and put my phone away. Leaving her wanting will only make tomorrow all the more exciting. The pull between us is explosive and I know it will be an interesting day. Of course, Zelda has better things to do than spending her life playing Santa but still, I'd quite happily put up with Christmas all year round if it means that she will stay at Bergman's.

I'm still wallowing in the afterglow of tonight and I can't remember the last time I had so much fun. She really did turn my apathy for Christmas around and I feel like creating some atmosphere in this awfully depressing room, so I light the three big candles sitting on Shelley's nightstand. We're not actually allowed candles in our dorm room, but Shelley was adamant when she brought them in, claiming the world is a better place with a hint of cinnamon. Then I turn on the string lights over her bed and smile as they create a cozy atmosphere, their glow casting soft shadows over the walls.

My copy of 'The Ultimate Guide to the MBE' is on the floor next to my bed and as I crawl back under the covers, I open the section on constitutional law and start reading. It's not exactly relaxing nighttime material, but until I pass my bar exam, it will have to do. Zelda is constantly on my mind, and as I try to take in what I'm reading, fantasies keep flooding back to me.

About an hour later, a soft knock on the door startles me. "Who is it?" I yell, not bothering getting out of bed. "Shelley's not here." I assume it's either one of her friends or some drunk student knocking on the wrong door as I rarely get visitors.

"I'm not looking for Shelley; it's Lucy I'm after." The voice seems to belong to an old man but there's something familiar in the tone. "It's Santa, I've heard you've been a naughty girl."

I let out a chuckle and clutch my hand to my chest, noting my heart is racing. "Santa? Just wait a second, I'm coming," I yell, then jump out of bed and quickly check my reflection in the mirror. Not that there's any time to do anything about my appearance; my hair is messy and I'm makeup free. Looking for something to cover myself up with, I grab my red negligée from my underwear drawer and put it on before opening the door.

"Sorry. Were you sleeping?" Zelda leans against the doorpost and glances inside before her eyes roam over me and settle on my cleavage.

"No, I was reading. And thinking of you," I add, pushing my chest forward as I tilt my head and smile seductively.

"Good. Because I was thinking of you too." She smirks and lets herself in, then closes the door behind her and drops the jute sack she was carrying on the floor, wasting no time as she pushes me against the wall. The snowflakes on her red hat and those nestled in her wig are melting fast, trickling down her face. When she pulls down her beard, a droplet runs over her mouth, following the beautiful curve of her upper lip. Although the idea has been on my mind, I never expected her to show up here unannounced. It's one thing to cross town in heavy snow but getting past the security guard without a key card is close to impossible in my experience.

"How did you—" My words are smothered by her mouth as she kisses me passionately, her lips and tongue taking me in a hungry frenzy. It feels incredible to be craved like this, to be desired and longed for. Knowing I've been on her mind until she couldn't stand it anymore makes me want to rip her costume off, but she stops me when I try to do so.

"Hands off Santa," she says in her groggy Santa voice, stepping away from me to inspect my room again. "One of my little helpers told me you've been a naughty girl. And I see you haven't cleaned up your mess."

I get what she's doing here, and I follow her gaze with an amused smile, noting the room is actually pretty tidy, apart from a pair of panties on the floor. "It's not that bad, is it, Santa?" I say in an innocent tone.

Zelda picks up the black, lace panties and dangles them in front of me. "What about these?" She uses her teeth to pull off one of her white gloves and runs her hand underneath my negligée and over my waxed pussy. "Shouldn't you be wearing them?"

"Should I?" I retort with a mischievous look, my breath hitching as she skims my clit.

"Every girl should be wearing underwear and you're not." She crosses her arms in front of her chest and the way she looks at me makes me squirm. I want her hand back where it was, but she's clearly in no rush and I will have to be patient. "Only bad girls walk around without panties on campus, so what are we going to do about that?"

"I don't know," I whisper, licking my lips as I shoot her a daring look. Since her confession about dorm room fantasies, I'm aware that simply being here is turning her on. Seeing me in nothing but my saucy negligée seems to have heightened her arousal as her eyes are so full of dark desire that I barely dare to meet them. I know exactly where this is heading and I'm trembling as I await my punishment.

Zelda takes off her other glove and sits on the edge of my bed, then taps her lap. "Come here and lay yourself over my knees."

Her command leaves no room for negotiation and a glowing ball of anticipation expands in my core. Settling myself over her lap, I'm baffled by how much this is turning me on. I wonder how she knew I was up for a spanking before I knew it myself. What gave it away? Did I come across as submissive? I really didn't think I had. Was it my reaction to her earlier teasing? If it's that easy to see through me, I really need to work on my game as I'll need to be on top form when arguing in court.

"Mmm..." Zelda pulls up the fabric of my negligée, baring my behind. I feel exposed, lying facedown over her lap and for a moment, I feel a hint of internal struggle—the little voice in my head telling me I'm kinky if I'm into this. I suppose I may have giggled if one of my friends had told me they were into roleplay; it's just always seemed ridiculous to me. As soon as she runs her hand over my cheeks though, all doubts fade and the delicious ache between my thighs intensifies while I moan at her caress.

"Are you enjoying this, Lucy?" she asks, slapping me hard on my left butt cheek.

I gasp and cry out, then reach for my pillow, hoping it will dampen the noise if I bury my face in it. Her fingers skim my pussy from behind and I spread my legs a little, just before she strikes me again on my other cheek. And again, and again. Harder and harder. Groaning into the pillow, I wallow in the conflicting sensation of the initial pain and the delicious glow that follows. The mouth-watering spanking is making me so wet that I suspect she can see my pussy glistening in the candlelight.

"Are you enjoying this? Answer me."

"Yes," I say through ragged breaths, my hands fisting the pillow while I bite into the cotton cover.

Zelda stops abruptly and the room turns silent. Caressing my sore skin, she leans sideways to whisper in my ear. "More or do you want me to stop?"

I need a moment to think about it. My behind is stinging and I'm pretty sure it's glowing red, but the effect is astounding, and I think I'm about to climax from this alone. Finally, I nod to acknowledge my consent.

"I can't hear you."

"Yes," I mumble into the pillow, then brace myself for more.

Another hard swat, and another, even harder. I clench my teeth and she stops, just as I'm about to ask her to. Then her fingers skim over my wetness and she moans as she enters me from behind, penetrating me slowly with two fingers.

"Fuck!" I yell as release starts to build inside me. When I

lift my hips, she slaps me with her other hand, and pushes me back down until I'm lying still.

"God, Lucy. You're so ready to be fucked." Zelda adds a third finger and I moan louder into the pillow as she moves in and out of me faster, hooking her fingers and hitting just the right spot. Unable to keep still any longer, I wiggle over her lap and she finally lets me drown in my fierce orgasm.

My face is flushed and I'm panting when I finally straighten myself and straddle her. I must look pretty bewildered because she chuckles as she brushes a lock of hair away from my face. Wrapping my arms around her neck, I take a moment to reflect. I can't believe I just let go like that, but it felt incredible. Going by the self-satisfied expression on Zelda's face, she's very pleased that I did. "That was…" I stop myself there because I'm unable to come up with the right word to describe how she just made me feel. I'm buzzing and on a high, and very, very eager to please her in return.

Pushing her down into the mattress, I pull down her red pants and start unbuttoning her jeans that she's wearing underneath. "Do you know what girls in dorm rooms do?" I ask mischievously.

"I have an idea."

I pull down her jeans and boxers while she takes off her hat and wig. Zelda licks her lips as I get off the bed and kneel before her, spreading her legs apart.

"Oh God!" When I run my tongue through her wetness, she covers her face with her hands and jerks her hips up. "You're so good at that." Sucking in a breath through her teeth, she grabs my hair and lifts me back up. "But I need to stop you there for a moment."

I frown, worried that I'm doing something wrong. "What is it?"

"From what I've heard, this is not what girls do in dorm rooms." Her grin puts me at ease, and I tilt my head as I get up on the bed.

"Then what do they do?"

Zelda takes off the big, black Santa belt, opens her red jacket and clips off the fake belly she's wearing. Holding me by the hips, she beckons me to turn around so I'm straddling her reverse cowboy style. "I think you know, Lucy. Being on Santa's naughty list and all..."

I chuckle as I shuffle back toward her face and bend forward to take her pussy into my mouth again. The moment she sinks her tongue into me, our combined pleasure causes the bed to shake, and lapping and sucking at her clit, I make her moan into my flesh. Her muffled cries drive me insane and her tongue inside me is already sending me to greater heights again. We're locked in the most intimate way, climbing together, feeding on each other's needs.

The circling of my tongue sends Zelda over the edge and as she parts her lips to moan against my pussy, I find release too, shuddering while I continue to feast on her. We're loud, chasing pleasure without holding back, and as I find my breath again and start to relax, I snuggle my cheek against her thigh. Breathing in her scent, I know I need her in my life.

23

Zelda makes me feel safe, and lying in the crook of her arm, I find myself telling her something I never talk about. "My father left when I was six." I'm not sure why I'm suddenly opening up to her, but I think I want her to know why I do what I do and why I take it so seriously. But most of all, I want her to know me.

"I'm sorry to hear that," she whispers, her expression genuine but not pitiful. I like that about Zelda; she seems real. But then again, she is an actress so I suppose I can't be sure of anything with her.

"Yeah. I remember waiting for him at home on Christmas Eve. He was away for business a lot, or so my mother thought. It was the first time in months he would be home for a full week, and I was super excited to have both my parents there. Anyway, he said he was still working on a case—he was a lawyer—but he promised to be home for Christmas." I bite my lip as I lift my gaze to meet Zelda's. "He never came, and I never saw him again."

"Jesus, Lucy. That's horrible. I get why you're not a fan of

Christmas now; I'm sorry if I put you through anything that conjured up sad feelings or…"

"No, it's fine. The thing is, it doesn't upset me anymore. You made me realize that today."

Zelda nods as she strokes my cheek. "What I don't get is why you want to become a lawyer too. Why do you still look up to him if he did that to you and your mom…"

"It's not like that." I hesitate and let out a long sigh. "I want to become a lawyer to nail guys like my father. But before you think I suffer from some sort of revenge complex; I want you to know I'm not looking for retribution. Instead, I want to help people like my mom. You see, my mother was a poor immigrant. She didn't come from a wealthy background like him, and she didn't have the support network of family here in New York. She worked as a seamstress for a high-end tailor when she met him. Her job was to measure him up when he came in to order a suit." I pause, imagining my mom in her younger years. She only told me the story of her life once, but I remember it word for word. "My father thought she was cute, he asked her out, and that's when their romance started. Then my mother fell pregnant. I wasn't planned but I know she never regretted having me. My father never gave me that impression either, but that only proves you never know what goes on inside someone's head. Anyway, I was young and just grateful to have him around every now and then so my memories may not be that reliable."

"Were they married?" Zelda asks.

"Yes, they got married when I was born, but he made her sign a prenup. At the time, he told her his parents had insisted but she never actually met them. Still, she didn't think much of it as she loved him and just assumed that they'd stay together forever. She didn't even read it," I say with regret. "According to my mom, they were happy for a couple of years, but my father started spending more and more time away from home. Much later, after he'd left, she found out that he'd met someone else and had another family while he was still with her. She never got over the betrayal, but the worst thing was that she got nothing after the divorce and had to start all over again."

"Fuck." Zelda winces. "Why didn't she take legal action?"

"She didn't have the means to do that. Mom could barely keep her head above water, paying the bills on the rental while suddenly being a single mom, let alone pay for legal counselling. Suing George—that's my dad's name—wasn't a priority for her then. Instead, she found a job after being a stay-at-home mom for six years, and we moved into a tiny studio in Brooklyn." I swallow hard as I feel my eyes sting with tears. "I'm sorry, I haven't cried in years and I have no idea why I suddenly feel so emotional."

"Don't apologize." Zelda takes me in her arms and hugs me tight. "It's good to talk about things." She kisses my forehead and runs a hand through my hair. "It's okay to be angry and sad. Anyone would be in your situation."

"It's not about me," I say. "Yes, he left us and that hurt me, but it was much harder for me to see my mom struggle, to see her so broken. For a while, she worked three jobs to keep us going; she's still working two jobs. That's why we don't celebrate Christmas together; we never have. And that's why I'm so focused on my future. I want to give her a comfortable life while helping women who are in the position that she was all those years ago."

There's a long silence before Zelda speaks again. "I understand why you're the way you are now," she says. "No wonder you put work over your own happiness."

"I don't do that," I argue, wiping at my cheeks. I'm still baffled that I've just opened up to her so fully, but it feels good that she knows this about me now.

"Yes, I think you do." Zelda grabs the jute bag from the floor next to the bed, takes out a single red rose and hands it to me. "But, Lucy, maybe it's time that you open up to romance in your life. Because right now, you're far too skeptical to ever be truly happy."

"Thank you." I take it and smile through my tears as I inhale deeply against the silky petals. "But I'm quite happy the way I am." My eyes move to the burning candles on Shelley's nightstand and although I know Zelda's right, I'm not ready to admit that to myself. "Tell me your story," I say. "Why are you such a hopeless romantic?"

Zelda laughs. "I'm not that bad, am I?"

"Yes, you are." I hold up the rose and she shrugs.

"Okay, okay. I just love being in love; I can't help it."

"Have you ever been truly in love?" I ask.

"Twice." I think I see a hint of regret in her eyes, but she swiftly collects herself. "It wasn't meant to be."

"What do you mean by that?"

Zelda takes a moment to consider her answer. "Well, let's just say we weren't compatible."

"In what way?" I'm aware that I sound like I'm interrogating her, but I want to understand her, and after I've just opened up—which I never do—it's only fair that she does the same.

Zelda trails a finger over my breasts, making my nipples rise to attention. "They weren't into sex as much as I am. A lifetime is long, and a life without amazing sex isn't an option for me. Don't get me wrong; they weren't bad in bed, and anyway, that would never be a reason for me to end a relationship. But they just weren't very interested in the physical aspect and after a year, that part of our relationship just died out. It took a little longer the second time, but still, we both realized we were just friends in the end." She locks her eyes with mine. "I'm a very sexual being. I'm sure you know what I mean, as you seem to be just as hungry for more."

I nod. "I know what you mean, although I had no idea I was so into sex until recently."

"You didn't?" Zelda's eyes narrow as she regards me. "I figured you were an extremely sexual creature, with the way you move, the lingerie you wear..." She smiles. "Not to mention the fact that you showed up on my doorstep without even knowing me."

"That's not really me though," I say, running a hand over her cheek. Her face is so alluring it takes my breath away, and I can't stop looking at her. "Sure, I love expensive lingerie; it makes me feel good about myself, even if no one sees it. It was only ever just for me. And showing up on someone's doorstep for sex isn't something I would normally do; not in a sober state anyway. But I'll gladly admit that I've never enjoyed sex as much as I have with you." I hesitate before I continue but decide to just spill the truth. "Seriously, nothing compares."

"I'm flattered and I feel the same." Zelda flicks her tongue over her lips and the simple action is so sensual that it makes me want to kiss her again. She has this magic ability to make me ache with longing each time she looks at me. I've never been a sucker for flattery but with her, I'm a puddle at the slightest attention she gives me. "So, you agree we have a special connection?"

"Yeah, I'm pretty sure our chemistry is off the charts." I inch closer, wallowing in her body heat. "So, what you're saying is that sex is important to you in a long-term relationship?"

"Very. Some may disagree and I know I'm on the extreme side of the scale but to me, sex is the very core of intimacy."

"I suppose so." My hand is drawn to Zelda's thigh and I trace her soft skin up to the curve of her hip, then continue toward the inside of her thigh. The path of goose bumps that suddenly appear makes me smile. "What's your background?" I ask. "Since you're a hopeless romantic and all." I draw the last sentence out in a teasing tone, but I actually like that she's so different from me. "What are your parents like? You never told me much about them, apart from calling them old hippies."

Zelda smiles and catches my hand before it disappears between her legs. "My parents are both artists; my father's a writer and my mother's a singer. They named me after Zelda Fitzgerald, a novelist, painter and the first American flapper."

"I can't imagine you as a flapper," I say with a chuckle. "Are they still happy together?"

"Yes, very. I grew up in a shared household not far from here, where we lived with three actors and two other authors. We weren't rich, but everyone supported each other in doing what they loved most. I suppose it was a commune in a way. My dad ended up being quite successful with his writing and my parents are fairly wealthy now, even though he never did it for the money. My mom still sings in nightclubs, simply because she loves to sing." Zelda winks. "She likes the attention too and honestly; I think she's addicted to applause. But she deserves it; she's good."

"So you got your voice from your mother?"

"We sound totally different, but listening to her made me want to sing when I was younger. She looked so happy on stage, and I feel that same spark when I'm performing."

"Wow, your upbringing sounds so interesting."

"Yeah, it was fun, growing up like that, and my parents always encouraged me to follow my dreams. I had singing and dancing lessons from an early age and I loved movies and theatre so when it came to planning my future, I thought, why not follow my passion?" Zelda shrugs. "After college, I was lucky to get the scholarship for Tisch, and as they say the rest is history."

"And you've been acting ever since?"

"Pretty much. I graduated when I was twenty-six, and I'm almost thirty-seven now."

"Oh." I prop my head on my hand and study her. "I thought you were much younger."

"Nope. Musicals keep me young. Rehearsals are hard and physically challenging and being on stage six days a week gives me endless energy so that helps me stay in shape. If I'm lucky, I'll still have a good twenty years left. A theatre career has more longevity than a TV or film career, because unlike those options I don't have to look perfect and young on camera."

"Your parents must be so proud of you."

"They are and I feel blessed to have them. It wasn't always perfect, you know. My mother had an on-off affair for a couple of years and it nearly broke my father's heart. But they worked through it eventually and now they're happier than ever." Zelda's features soften and I can tell by the loving expression in her eyes that she's very close to her parents. "There's just something beautiful about growing old with someone; sharing a life, a lifetime."

"Is that what you're looking for?"

"Yes, that's what I want and I'm not ashamed to admit it."

"Well, I doubt you'll find it by telling random women you want to fuck them," I joke.

Zelda laughs. "Hey, as I said, sex is very important to me, whether I'm in a relationship or not." She looks at me pensively. "So, what is it that you want?"

Although she probably doesn't mean it that way, it sounds like a loaded question to me. "I want a career, I say. A job that will give me a decent income and at the same time, give me satisfaction. As a divorce lawyer it will be great knowing I can nail guys like my father and help women like my mother. Or of course it might be the reverse, I add. It's not always the women who suffer."

Zelda nods. "Is love not in the picture?"

I hesitate, then shake my head. "A serious, long-term relationship has never been high on my priority list. I'm not sure if I believe in everlasting love."

"But you believe in passion. Don't those two go hand in hand?"

"For someone in the arts like you maybe, but for me it's just good sex." As I say it, I'm not so sure how I feel anymore because Zelda has turned my world upside down and it's confused the hell out of me. For a moment, I consider telling her that but then my deep-rooted skepticism kicks in again and I let out a long sigh. "So no, I don't believe in everlasting love."

"That must be a sad existence." Zelda looks a little sorry for me and it makes me uneasy.

"No, it's not," I say, putting on a brave smile. "It's predictable and comfortable and just the way I like it."

Zelda frowns and I can almost hear her thinking out

loud, her instincts telling her this can only ever end in disaster. "Okay. Well, it's late. I guess I'd better head home."

As I open my mouth to protest, no words come out. I want to ask her to stay the night, but I don't, and so she gets up, puts her Santa costume back on and blows me a kiss before leaving.

24

It's hard to get our panic buyers to leave at four p.m. Some are still grabbing what they can while security guards are breathing down their necks, gently ushering them toward the tills. I've hardly had time to talk to Zelda today, and she's been equally busy, with mothers dumping their husbands and kids by her sleigh while they rush through Bergman's for last-minute purchases like the apocalypse is coming. Seeing her in her costume reminds me of last night, and I've been permanently turned on since I arrived this morning.

Even though there was no sign of irritation from Zelda's side, the way we left things last night bothers me. I don't want her to think sex is all I'm after, but then again, I don't know what it is that I want. Since I didn't ask her to stay the night, she may have drawn her own conclusions. As soon as she left, I regretted letting her go, and I spent the rest of the night racking my brain over why I'm so scared of getting close to her while missing the warmth of her body next to me. The answer never came but the feeling remains; I need her.

Telling myself to stop overthinking things, I finally log out of the system and head for the restrooms to put on the spare elf costume that Andy gave me. As I put on the ridiculous red and white striped socks, I realize they're actually knee socks, so I pull them over the green jersey pants that fit me like leggings. I'm not sure if I'm supposed to wear them like this but at least it makes the costume look a little sexier and I have a feeling Zelda will appreciate the effort I'm making. Then I put on the sneakers I've brought with me and top them off with the boot covers. The bells on my feet make me laugh as I hop around in front of the mirror, mimicking the way I imagine elves to move. The green top with red collar is not much better, but I tug the black belt that comes with it tight around my waist to create an hour-glass shape. Pulling the matching green and red hat with attached elf-ears over my hair, I decide it's the best I can make of it, apart from a little red lipstick.

All the Santas and elves are gathered in the restaurant on the sixth floor, ready to collect the packages that have been prepared for them. Dozens of jute bags fill the tables that have been pulled together in a long rectangle. The event coordinator is standing behind it, handing out the goods to the designated teams.

I'm the last one to join them so I sneak in quietly. Although I'm aware that I look beyond silly in the green elf costume, it's a small price to pay for spending time with Zelda. Besides that, Andy is happy with the arrangement as he'll get paid while I do his work, so I doubt he'll be causing any trouble now. I scan the row of Santas from behind, trying to work out which one is Zelda. They're all wearing the exact same costume provided by Bergman's but it's her posture that gives her away. Her relaxed stance, hands folded over her false stomach and the way her broad shoulders shake as she laughs sends a wave of ripples to my core.

"What are you doing here?" she whispers when I tap her shoulder. She looks confused and stares me up and down, no doubt wondering why I'm wearing an elf costume before snickering into the palm of her hand.

"Surprise," I say, keeping my voice down so I won't draw attention to myself. Although it's highly unlikely the coordinator will ask me for an ID, I'm still doing something underhand by passing for Andy and I don't want to get caught. "I'm your little helper." Placing my index finger over my lips, I shoot her a wink.

From the look on Zelda's face, she couldn't be happier. "Am I dreaming? I can't believe this is happening; I mentally prepared myself for hours in hell with Andy." Her dazzling smile widens as she runs a hand down my back and pinches my ass. "Instead I got the sexiest elf in this room."

Holding back a giggle, I pretend to listen to the last instructions before we're each given five jute bags with an information sheet that contains the addresses, the kid's names, their interests and one or two anecdotes provided by the parents that will help Zelda come across as a convincing Santa.

"Have they arranged drivers or are we taking a cab?" I ask as we carry the bags out of the restaurant.

"You have no idea about any of this, do you?" Zelda raises a brow at me. "Did Andy not give you the brief from the agency?"

"No. He just shoved the costume in my hands and left," I say with a shrug.

Zelda laughs. "Okay. I'll talk you through it in more detail on the way, but you'll be happy to know that we're delivering the presents in a Christmas sleigh come float. Our district is Brooklyn and we're taking a cab to meet the driver there."

"Really?" My eyes widen and I feel genuine excitement to do this now.

"Yeah. It will be fun."

Noting the other elves are wearing a white turtleneck under their costumes and most likely a pair of thick leggings, I silently curse Andy for holding back undoubtedly valuable information. "Should I grab my coat before we leave?" I subtly brush the back of my hand against Zelda's, and she hooks her pinkie through mine.

"Don't worry," she says with a smile. "We'll have blankets in the back, and I'll make sure to keep you warm."

25

Zelda and I are sitting in the back of the white sleigh, snuggled under warm blankets, and our float is being driven by a guy dressed in a black suit and tie—all he needs are some shades and he could well pass for a secret service agent assigned to look out for Santa tonight. Our sleigh is decorated with tiny white string lights and from a speaker behind us, Christmas carols are playing. I'm in such a great mood that I find myself singing along to them while waving at pedestrians who raise their cameras to snap pictures of us. Truth be told, I've felt like I've been in a fairy-tale all week, but this experience trumps my wildest dreams.

Fluffy snowflakes fall from the dark sky, gently settling on every surface. I've never been in this part of Brooklyn but unlike I imagined, it's far from quiet here. Families are building snowmen; children are chasing each other in snowball fights and residents are sitting in their front yards or along the street drinking hot apple cider while catching up with their neighbors. The farther we venture into the suburbs, the more elaborate the decorations get, and I can hardly believe my eyes as our float turns into 84th street.

"What has happened here?" I say, gawking at the ostentatious decorations as we pass the first couple of houses. I've heard that the residents here see the holidays as a yearly competition, but I never imagined anything like this.

"It's madness," Zelda agrees, following my gaze to the over-the-top displays in the front yards. The large houses that line the street look like theme parks of their own, the roofs and facades fully covered in bling. Archways of lights lead up to their front doors, some blinking and moving like light shows. "I bet this is visible from outer space."

"No kidding," I mumble as my eyes flick from one yard to the other.

There's no end to the kitsch on display and the next row of houses looks even more spectacular. A dazzling array of snowmen, reindeer, elves, Christmas trees, candy canes and other giant paraphernalia cover the lawns, now white from the snow that has been falling non-stop over the past twenty-four hours. We even pass a working Ferris wheel with five bucket seats in one of the front yards. Laser beams shoot from the frame as it turns, projecting 'season's greetings' on the roof of the house.

"Two kids, right?" I ask, noting that I'm actually feeling a little nervous about playing an elf. I'm no actor and although Zelda has assured me that I can leave the talking to her, I'm worried I won't be convincing enough.

"Yes. Edward and Danielle. Three and four." Zelda checks her file once more and gives me a smile. "Don't worry, you'll be great."

Arriving at the house, we're greeted by the biggest inflatable Santa I've ever seen. He's waving his hands and a deep disembodied voice blasts 'ho ho ho' from a speaker somewhere on the driveway making us jump. The float comes to a stop and the driver opens the door for us.

"I'll wait here," he says, producing an insulated flask from his satchel.

As we unload the presents, I can't help but chuckle when I spot the neon sign that says: 'The Richards family. Lighting it up since 2012' I can already imagine the kind of people who live here.

"I know," Zelda says as if reading my mind. "Welcome to the burbs where they rip out the trees and name the streets after them."

Sarcasm aside, clearly no level of restraint has been practiced here. The house is blanketed in lights, not an inch of it left undecorated. The way it's illuminated reminds me of a rocket about to take off. A two-storey snowman is holding an arrow that points to the door with the words, 'Santa, this way'.

This isn't for the kids, I realize then. The parents have gone all-out to have the best display in the neighborhood, and now they want everyone to see that they have a real Santa coming in too. A Santa in a sleigh bearing the Bergman's logo.

"It must have taken them months to do this," I say.

Zelda shrugs. "If they can afford the gold package from Bergman's they can undoubtedly afford staff to set it up for them."

"True." I've never felt envious of my friends at school who had a big Christmas at home but now that I'm here, it hits me how incredibly divided the world is. This life is so far from mine that it's hard to imagine kids growing up in such flamboyant wealth.

The Richards' Christmas mission is a success; the neighbors are crossing their lawns to admire our sleigh, others stand on their doorsteps, wrapped in robes. The envious looks on some of their faces tell me they will do everything in their power to make this happen for their own kids next year. Others look worried, as the bar has simply been set too high.

Before we get the chance to knock, a little girl has already opened the door and the beaming smile on her face makes me remember why I'm here.

"You must be Danielle," Zelda's says, kneeling down to shake her hand.

"Santa…" The bewilderment in her sweet high-pitched voice is endearing as her big brown eyes stare up at Zelda in awe. Her brother joins her in the doorway, jumping and shrieking with joy.

Zelda laughs her deep, roaring Santa laugh and turns her attention to the boy. "And you must be Edward." She pats my shoulder. "This is Santa's helper, Lucy. Can you guys go and get your parents? We have something for you both."

26

————

Four hours and many happy children later, we're passing through Prospect Park on our way back to the pick-up point. I managed to fall into the role of elf and now have a whole new gained respect for actors. It wasn't easy but it was fun and although it's been years since I was a babysitter, I haven't lost my touch with kids.

"Somewhere you'd like to go?" the driver asks us. "Your event manager booked me until eleven to cover emergencies, so you still have close to an hour left on the reservation."

"Isn't that diner where your mom works around here somewhere?" Zelda asks.

"Yeah, it's not far. Why? Are you in the mood for chili?"

"I'm always in the mood for chili." Zelda laughs and shakes her head. "But that's not why I asked. What time does she finish?"

I purse my lips as I try to remember what Mom told me about her Christmas schedule. "A little after ten, I think."

"Want to give her a ride home? It would be a nice surprise and it sure beats the subway, right?" Zelda checks the time again and raises her voice so the driver can hear her. "Any chance you could make a quick stop at a diner nearby and drop us off in..." She frowns and turns to me. "Your mom lives in Brooklyn, right?"

"Yeah, on this side of Bushwick."

"Right. That's it. Bushwick. It shouldn't be more than half an hour from here."

"But that's out of the way for him," I whisper.

The driver takes a moment to think it through, clearly not looking forward to going that far out of his way. "How about this," he says. "I'll do that for you tonight, if you guys drop by my kids tomorrow before we start."

"Deal." Zelda shoots him a grin and gives him a thumbs-up. "You have my number, just text me your address and anything I need to know about them."

"Are you sure you're okay with picking up my mom?" I ask her. "You must be tired after a long day and last night was—"

"No, I'm feeling great," Zelda interrupts me. She puts an arm around me and pulls me close while she directs the driver toward the diner.

The look of surprise on Marjorie and my mom's faces as they see Santa and his elf arriving on a sleigh is priceless, and as they peer through the window it's clear they don't recognize me until I take off my hat and wave at them.

My mother gawks at me incredulously, then bursts into laughter before she unlocks the door to come and meet me outside.

"Good heavens, what have you been up to, Lucy?" Then her eyes shift to the distinct logo on the side of the sleigh. "Are you working?"

"Something like that. We're doing the personal deliveries. Are you busy?"

My mother shakes her head, still laughing at my outfit. "I'm almost done. We've just closed the kitchen, but I can box up some chili for you to take home, if you'd like?" She looks up at Zelda, who has removed her beard. "And you're Lucy's friend. Zelda, right?"

"That's right, ma'am." Zelda gives her a wave. "But we didn't come for the chili, although it was really, really good the other night. We were wondering if you'd like a ride home instead."

"You're giving me a ride home? In that?" Mom looks like she doesn't believe Zelda and turns her attention to me. "Is she for real, Lucy?"

Marjorie, who has been flirting with the driver, rushes inside, grabs my mother's bag and her coat and hands them to her. "Here, give me that apron, Maria," she says with no room left for argument in her tone. When my mother doesn't immediately get in, she gives her a smack on her behind and laughs. "Hurry up. I'm sure they don't have all night and you don't get to ride in a Bergman's sleigh every day. A Bergman's sleigh!" she repeats, staring at the logo as if it's the holy grail. "I'll close up; hubby's picking me up so it's all good."

"Good heavens," my mother mumbles again, looking thoroughly impressed as she sits back in the comfortable blanket covered seats in the sleigh. "Thank you, girls. This is wonderful." She smiles at Zelda. "I suppose I have you to thank for this? So, tell me honestly. Are you two dating?"

Zelda opens her mouth to answer, then closes it again, leaving the decision to me. I guess we're dating, but as we haven't really discussed it, I'm not quite ready to admit that to my mother.

"Just friends, Mom," I say, immediately regretting it. I've dressed up as an elf just to be with Zelda. If that doesn't mean it's more than casual, I don't know what does. I subtly brush my hand against Zelda's and give it a squeeze as if to say I'm sorry.

"Sure, honey." My mother shoots me a wink, clearly not convinced. "It would be terribly romantic though if you were. It's Christmas Eve, love is all around..." She lets out a dramatic sigh as she glances out over the snowscape. Even in the less gentrified areas of Brooklyn, everyone's made an effort to decorate.

"I don't think I've ever heard you utter the words 'love' or 'Christmas' in a positive context, let alone combined. Are you sure you're okay?" I ask her.

"Absolutely." Mom rakes a manicured hand through her hair and puts her arm around me. "I'm sorry we never celebrated Christmas when you were younger."

"It's okay, Mom. I know why we didn't, and I was never comfortable with this time of year either."

"Well, it's still not fair; it's something I've been thinking about lately. I could at least have made an effort, instead of having you seated at that table in the diner on Christmas Eve. I should have made better memories for you instead of ignoring Christmas altogether. That must have only reminded you of what happened." She pauses and shoots Zelda an apologetic look. "Forgive me. This is not the time or place for a heart to heart with my daughter; I guess I'm getting sentimental in my old age but it's just so sweet that you're doing this for me that I..." She stops herself as her eyes well up.

"Don't worry about it. Isn't this what Christmas is all about? Connecting to your loved ones?" Zelda reaches over my lap and squeezes my mother's hand. "Lucy told me about her father. I'm very sorry that happened to you both."

My mother smiles back at her. "Thank you, honey. The

past is the past and I try not to fret over it anymore, but I have come to realize that I did many things wrong when Lucy was younger." She leans into me and I place a soft kiss on her cheek. "We never had fun together, I was always at work. Hell, Lucy was always there too, whenever she wasn't at school. But this is nice, and I think we should do more things together. I'm not getting any younger and I'd like to have some fun while I can," she continues. "Perhaps I set the wrong example for you. You're always locked up in that dorm room when you're not at work."

"You didn't, Mom." I turn to her and smile. "I'm fine and happy and you were an amazing mother. You still are." I don't know what's caused this change but she's not the mother I know right now. She's a happier, more present and emotional version of herself. Suddenly I feel worried. "You're not sick, are you?"

"Me?" My mother shakes her head. "No, I'm as healthy as they come." She points to a communal Christmas tree in front of a run-down apartment block. "Don't you think everything looks so much prettier, covered in snow? I never liked this street, but it looks charming now..."

"Yeah, it's very pretty." If tonight was magical, this is entirely surreal. I'm sitting between my crush and my mother in the back of a sleigh being driven through the snowy streets of Brooklyn on a float. My mother is opening up about her feelings, and I'd almost go as far as to say that we've both caught the Christmas spirit. "Are you working tomorrow?" I ask. Normally I wouldn't worry about her being alone over the holidays but after what she's just said, I wonder if she needs company.

"Yes, I'm doing the early shift. And after that I'm volunteering at the soup kitchen. There's one behind the diner."

I know exactly which soup kitchen she means. Mom

must think I've forgotten about it, but I vividly remember going there with her twice, when life was at its hardest. I remember because she cried, and mom rarely cries, apart from tonight, and I wonder what's caused the change. "You're volunteering?" I pause. "That's very sweet of you. It's just that you work so much as it is and—"

"No, I like doing it," she says. "A friend of mine has just replaced the previous manager and he made me want to volunteer, so I was there last week and decided to come back."

"Which friend?" I ask.

"Oh, just someone who comes in the diner a lot. You don't know him."

I'll be dammed if that isn't a blush on her cheeks and when she avoids my gaze, it suddenly clicks. I note her nails are painted another color yet again. She's also paid extra attention to her hair and makeup, and she's even wearing small gold studs in her ears. "Are you seeing him?"

"Seeing him?" Her lips pull into a small smile and she looks from Zelda to me and back before cheekily replying. "No, we're just friends."

27

We're back at Zelda's apartment and we've had a long shower together that was hot on all levels. Buttoning up the flannel shirt she gave me to wear, I feel giddy and even a little emotional as I come out of the bathroom. She's cranked up the heating, lit candles and laid the table. Just as I'm about to comment on the room's romantic setting, the doorbell rings.

"That will be the food," she says, buzzing the delivery guy up. "You must be starving; I know I am." She tips him and hands me the bags to unpack. "I didn't know what you liked so I just ordered a bit of everything."

"Zelda, you shouldn't have done this..." My mouth starts watering as I take out the cartons and breathe in the aroma of Thai food. "But yes, I am hungry."

She comes up behind me and kisses my neck. "I can't thank you enough for taking over from Andy. I've had so much fun with you tonight."

"Me too." I tilt my head and close my eyes as her lips linger on the nape of my neck. Her touch makes all my nerve endings buzz and my infatuation with her only seems to grow the more time we spend together. I suppose I expected it to fade; that's been the case with other women I've slept with in the past, but quite the opposite is true. "I should be the one thanking you though," I say. "For being so kind to my mom."

"Hey, I like your mom." Zelda places another kiss on my neck, then sits down opposite me. "And I'm happy for her; it's pretty clear that she's in love."

"You're right. Her new 'friend'," I say, making quote marks in the air, "must be quite something, the way she's suddenly oversharing in front of strangers."

"I don't mind." Zelda plates herself some food from one of the boxes, then passes it to me. "I like that she feels comfortable around me."

"Anyone would feel comfortable around you. You're just easy to be around."

"Are you calling me easy?" she jokes.

"Yes." I smile coyly. "In a good way."

We sample the selection of amazing dishes and discuss our favorite foods over dinner. It really is easy with her; I don't have to try hard or stress about anything because being myself is good enough. There's a weird new feeling in my belly and it's bigger than anything I understand. The more I hang out with Zelda, the more it grows, and I didn't know what it was at first, but tonight, I think I might have an idea. I care for her and I want to be near her. I respect her and I like her for everything she is. Frankly, she's the best thing that's happened to me in years, perhaps ever.

"Can I stay over tonight?" The words have left my lips before I've thought them through.

Zelda stops chewing and stares at me. Swallowing down her food, she nods. "Of course you can." I know she's pretending it's no big deal, but we both know it is. There's a sincere sparkle in her eyes when she adds, "I'd like that very much."

I stare back at her and feel like there are so many things I want to say but I don't know how to voice my feelings or where to even start. I have to say something though; I owe her that because what we shared wasn't just sex, no matter how hard I've tried to fool myself. I pause, hesitating before I say the first thing that comes to mind. "The timing may not be great, but I doubt I'll ever feel something like this again."

Zelda's fork drops to the table. I can tell I've caught her off guard once again, and I can only hope I haven't scared her off now. Her mind is churning, that much is clear, and her eyes narrow as if she's trying to work out if I really mean what I'm saying. She clears her throat, then leans in to take my hand. "Honestly," she says, "I've never felt anything like this before either. I wasn't sure if I even wanted to accept the job at Bergman's, but I had nothing better to do so I thought why not? And looking back, I can see it was the best decision I've ever made." She smiles, immediately putting me at ease. "I wouldn't have met you if I'd turned it down. Imagine that... I wouldn't have known you were out there."

"That's true. Imagine that..." I look into her eyes and there's a long silence between us. I'm not good at talking, but she makes me want to open up. Suddenly I feel like I need to know how we're moving forward because I don't want to lose her. "So, what are we going to do?" The simple sentence leaves me in a breathless whisper. It's frightening as it suggests more. It suggests the chance of a future, or a promise.

"What do you want to do?"

"I want more." I pause. "Not just more sex. I want to be with you."

"You want to be my girl?" Zelda asks.

"Your girl?" I giggle. "That sounds cute. I didn't think people still said that."

"I say it. I'm kind of crazy about you." Zelda looks adorable with a blush. Her fingers caress the palm of my hand. "Listen, I know things are going to be hectic, with your internships and me being on stage six days a week, but if we really want to, we can make this work."

"I know." My smile widens, and then I say the words I never thought I'd never say, astounding myself by how easily they roll off my tongue. "Then I'm your girl."

28

————

"Forget about the dishes." I'm about to get up to clear the table when Zelda puts her hands on my shoulders and pushes me back down. "I'll do that tomorrow." She pulls my hair to the side and kisses my neck. Gently at first, then hungrier as she roams a hand over my breasts.

Her breath is tickling my ear, and shivering from the sensation, I tilt my head and give in to her caress. Sucking at my sensitive flesh, she draws a long moan from my mouth. I know she's marking me, and I want to be marked. I'm her girl now.

"Come to bed with me," she whispers as she unbuttons my shirt. "I want to try something new."

After she slides the flannel fabric off my shoulders, I'm naked at the table, my body on high alert waiting for what's to come. "Something new?"

"You'll like it." Zelda takes my hand and guides me to the bed where I lie down. My hands are resting above my head on the pillow and my knees are together, slightly bent. She unties her robe and lets it fall down so she's naked before me, and I marvel at her toned frame, her full breasts and the strip of dark hair between her legs. I'm dying to touch her there, to taste her, and I'm dying to have her naked body on mine. Zelda has the ability to turn me into something primal and I don't think I'm capable of saying no to her. She's the sweetest temptation, the wildest adventure, the warmest blanket, the most delicious treat and satisfaction personified. When she says, 'you'll like it', I know I will.

She walks over to a chest of drawers against the wall next to the bed and takes out a blindfold and two long pieces of black satin. My pussy twitches and every muscle in by body tightens with anticipation. "I'm going to take you to higher places," she says, cocking her head to look at me as she gets on the bed. There's no hint of the dominatrix in her voice but from her dark expression I can tell that she's been looking forward to this.

"What are you going to do to me?"

"Take away one of your senses which should enhance the others. Zelda smiles and holds up the blindfold. "Are you okay with this?"

I simply nod and swallow hard as she places the blindfold over my eyes and pulls the elastic over my hair. My lashes flutter against the fabric when I blink, trying to see at least something, but the blindfold sits snug against my cheeks and doesn't let any light through. Already, I feel my heart accelerate with excitement.

"Can you see anything?" Zelda asks.

"No." I feel her move toward the top of the bed and tense when she takes my hands. Every action—even something as simple as this—feels scary because I can't see what she's doing, and I don't know what will happen.

"I'm not going to hurt you," she says in a reassuring tone. "Are you okay with being restrained?"

I nod again, so she ties my wrists together and when

she's done, I instinctively wiggle my hands to see if I can free myself, then realize that I'm helpless and utterly under her control. Adrenaline kicks in and my chest starts heaving but I like the visceral sensation it has created. She's right; my body feels more alive than ever, and I'm dripping wet, my limbs trembling while I await her actions. Nothing happens for long moments and I think she's looking at me to gauge my reaction. Zelda's warm hand lands between my breasts and I gasp at the unexpected touch. I chuckle at my response, because her caress is gentle and calm and there's no need to panic but being deprived of my eyesight, everything startles me. I'm like an animal in fight-or-flight mode, a ball of nerves, but they're the good kind of nerves. She keeps her hand there for a while, perhaps to calm me down.

"Your heart is beating really fast," she says. "Are you okay?"

"Yes," I whisper, then try to wiggle myself out of my bindings again.

"Just say stop and I'll untie you immediately." Zelda takes my hands and kisses me softly. "But I very much doubt you will." Her voice sounds incredibly sexy in my ear. Deep, calming, promising...

I turn my head and tilt my chin to meet her mouth again and she gives in, pressing them hard against mine. When she parts her lips and our tongues meet, my libido fires up like it's been torched. The kiss is so intense that we're both left breathless by the time Zelda pulls away from me and I take pleasure in knowing that she's very, very turned on too.

Again, I feel her move away, this time to the end of the bed. I hear noises but can't figure out what she's doing, and I know she has no intention of telling me. The element of surprise is stronger than I ever anticipated and it's leaving me so aroused that my breath hitches when she takes hold of my knees. Holding them, she waits for what seems like an eternity, then spreads them apart so slowly that I'm not sure if I can take this anymore. I know she's looking at me, seeing how swollen and throbbing I am.

"Stay still," she says before letting go of my knees. She fiddles with something and I hear a squirting sound. Remembering the lube she used to fuck me with in the utility room at Bergman's, my pussy aches with need. "You don't need this, but it will feel good," she says, as she positions herself between my legs.

Before she touches me, every part of my body and brain shuts down, like silence before a storm, awaiting the raging tempest that I know will follow. My hips shoot up and I groan as I feel the silky gel against my oversensitive lips. The conflicting sensations are incredible and as I shiver—caught in the throes of passion as her skilled fingers languorously explore my folds—my chill is replaced by a growing ball of fire that sends a tingling heat to my core... Exploring me while she rubs in the lube, I hear her chuckle at my response. I'm moaning, writhing, sighing, quivering, and it's impossible to lie still. Her hair tickles my skin as she places featherlight kisses on my thighs and my belly. Then she moves up to my breasts, her tongue tracing every inch of my body while she massages my pussy. I'm a wild mess. Zelda knows what she's doing and she's very, very good at it.

When she moves up to claim my mouth, I feel something between my legs and know she's wearing her strap-on. As she grinds into me, it drags through my folds and I'm afraid I'll come before she's even entered me. Her hands are in my hair, her breath heavy against my mouth. "This is going to be good," she whispers.

I arch my back and spread my legs wider, so ready for her to fuck me. Her weight on top of me is heavenly while her mouth devours mine. She enters me, slowly stretching me open in the most delicious way.

"How does that feel?" she whispers.

"It feels amazing."

"Good. I thought I'd give you your Christmas present early. Do you remember that other little thing I ordered from the adult department?"

I nod. "I've been wondering about that. It—" I gasp when something suddenly vibrates against my clit. "Oh... my... God..." I whisper through heavy breaths, embracing the stimulation that is like nothing I've ever felt before.

"Fuck!" Zelda cries. The battery-operated O-ring stimulates her clit too while she pushes into me. It immediately relaxes my muscles and I lift my hips to take her deeper. I want her as close against me as possible; I want all of her all over me.

I move with her, faster, wilder, deeper, and she fucks me harder, just long enough to bring me to the brink, then pulls back a little when we're about to explode.

"I want you to look at me while you come," she says, taking off my blindfold before pinning my hands above the pillow and slamming into me again. Sweat is pearling on her forehead and her pupils are dilated like holding back has short circuited her brain. Never in my life have I seen anything as sexy as Zelda right now and when I meet her eyes and nod, letting her know I can't wait any longer, she pushes deeper, tighter against me, making us crash and fall. Her need is powerful and all-consuming as she tenses and squeezes my hands while letting out a long, throaty cry that blends with the loud moans rising from deep within me. I scream her name and she repeats mine over and over until there is nothing but the sound of our ragged breathing.

The ring is still vibrating, making us both jerk every few

seconds, and the feeling is still so intense that I can't get enough. It's like she's unleashed a beast inside me that's been waiting to hunt and take what it wants. "Untie me," I say. "I want more."

"You want more, huh?" Zelda looks both smug and intensely satisfied as she pulls at the ties around my wrists to release me. "Why don't you show me what you want?"

I immediately reach for her silky soft hair and lace my fingers through it, then roll us over with the shaft still inside me. I straddle her and rock my hips, making her moan in pleasure.

"Holy fuck, that's amazing," she whispers, staring up at my naked body. Holding me by my hips, she lifts me up and spasms shoot through my pussy as the tension releases. I know what she wants and I'm going to give it to her.

Zelda licks her lips and her expression is lust filled as she watches the shaft disappear inside me again, little by little when I sink back. I sit down with my full weight and let her fill me up as she tilts her hips for me to take it even deeper. "Don't stop..." she whispers as I slowly roll my hips and grind down against her. "This is incredible." She looks like she's close again already and so am I.

I realize that I'm in control now, and she's at my mercy. As I stop moving just to tease her a little, her hands pull at my hips impatiently, desperate for me to release her. She's beautiful lying there; her eyes fluttering, and her brows furrowed. Full, perky breasts and hard nipples invite me to run my hands over them and it makes her shiver and moan when I do so. I can't hold back any longer as the vibrations are causing my pussy to clench around the shaft, so I lean forward and grind into her hard while I run my hands through her hair and kiss her.

The second time around is just as explosive. Our mouths

locked, our combined orgasms flowing through us, connecting us on all levels. It's like we're going through a cosmic, out of this world, experience together and our kiss is so passionate that I can't breathe. Aftershocks keep taking us by surprise and long moments pass before I finally ask Zelda to switch off the ring because I'm exhausted and can't take any more.

Breathing in the scent of her shampoo, I close my eyes and rest my forehead against hers, feeling incredibly close to her.

Zelda wraps her arms around me and smiles against my mouth and, as if on cue, we both laugh because it's hard to grasp how good we are together. Her laugh is warm and hearty, and the lyrical sound of it fills me with a whole new kind of happiness. Cupping my cheeks, her smile widens, and she tilts her head in the cutest way when she says, "Merry Christmas, baby."

29

"Merry Christmas, beautiful." My eyes flutter open and as I look into Zelda's blue eyes, I don't think I've ever felt this good in my life. Everything is warm and comfortable and her strong, sexy arms are wrapped tightly around me.

"Hey, you. Merry Christmas, sexy." I stretch out and kiss her, soft whimpers passing my lips as her hands roam over my naked body. Making out feels incredible in my sleepy state, like I'm still in a dream. It's slow and sensual; a dance of limbs entangled, and I don't know and don't care where she ends and I begin.

It's strange and wonderful to wake up next to her and although it was only one night, it feels like everything has changed.

"Are you ready to do the Christmas rounds with Santa?" she jokes.

"I am." I look out of the windows and feel excited to see that it's still snowing. Zelda yawns and is about to get up but I push her back down and kiss her forehead. "I'll make coffee," I say, then jump out of bed and put on her robe.

"Thank you, babe." Zelda pulls the covers up to keep herself warm. "Coffee in bed with my hot girlfriend; that's the best start to any Christmas Day I can think of."

I blush at the girlfriend comment and shoot her a wink. It's only really hitting me then that I really am her girlfriend, and that makes me even more elated. This incredible woman is mine and only mine, and I intend to do everything in my power to make this work.

Sore in all the right places, I roll my shoulders as I pass the floor to ceiling windows, and stopping myself there, I glance over the winter wonderland that is so pure it's hard to imagine we're in New York. The streets are still quiet and the smooth, cushiony white surface on the pavement is only broken up by a couple of footsteps and paw prints.

"The coffee machine is pretty straightforward," Zelda calls from across the room. "Just turn it on, press the bean grinder and select the type you want. The frother with milk is in the fridge."

As I find mugs and make coffee, I spot an old-fashioned radio on the counter and turn it on. Normally, Christmas songs would make my head hurt early in the morning or any time of day for that matter, but as the sound of a familiar tune fills the air, I'm amazed that I actually want to turn up the volume.

Zelda laughs. "What's gotten into you? Are you channeling your inner elf?"

"Maybe." I shoot her a grin and hum along to the song I only know the melody of. Not being used to this level of intimacy, I thought I might feel a little uncomfortable being here in her apartment after spending the night but quite the opposite is true. Christmas morning used to be a gloomy day for me when I was younger and since my late teens, it's just been like any other day of the year. But today feels special and I know that my mom is right. It's time that I put the past behind me and start making new Christmas memories. Happy ones, this time.

"Here you go." I hand Zelda her coffee and get back under the covers with her. I could stay here all day and sex is still on my mind, but we have to be dressed in an hour, ready to spread more Christmas joy in New York's suburbs.

"Thanks." Zelda flips through her file to check our schedule. "We're stopping off at the driver's house first, and after that we're doing eight households. It's going to be a long day."

"A long day sounds perfect as long as I'm with you," I hear myself say, then shake my head and chuckle, cringing at my sudden sentiment. I have no idea what's happened to me but I'm giddy and full of energy, so I'll take it.

"And of course, you can stay over again, if you want." Zelda looks at me sincerely as she raises a hand. "I don't want you to feel pressured of course; I just figured you might be more comfortable here than in your dorm room."

"It is nice here," I admit. "So, I might take you up on that offer." Despite the hesitation in my tone, my stomach is excitedly swirling at the prospect of another night with her. I arch a brow at her and shoot her a suggestive smile. "But you did say you had a thing for dorm rooms."

Zelda chuckles. "I do. In fact, I was thinking that—" Her phone rings and she quickly picks up. "Hey, this is Zelda." Her expression turns serious while she listens, and then she starts asking questions. "How? What happened? Is he going to be okay?" Listening again, she occasionally comments and repeats a street name before saying, "Of course Andy and I can do that. Send me the details and we'll pick up the goods. Thanks, Angel. Don't worry, we've got it covered."

"What's wrong?" I ask after she's hung up.

"One of the Santas had an accident last night. He slipped on ice during the deliveries so we have to cover for two of his stops and the other teams will take care of the rest."

"Poor man. Is he going to be okay?"

"Yeah. Angel, my agent, said he's broken his leg. It's sad for him as he won't be able to work for a while but at least it's nothing more serious. Bernie's a good guy; we were on stage together for a season." Zelda puts her phone away and finishes her coffee. "He was supposed to do a charity drop; Bergman's is donating part of their leftover Christmas stock to a homeless shelter in Manhattan, so we'll make that our last delivery. We'll go without the sleigh of course; but we have a driver who will meet us at the warehouse and take us there in a van."

"Sure. I'm pleased to hear Bergman's make charitable donations. I didn't know that."

"I didn't either, I just do what I'm told and don't ask questions." Zelda gets out of bed and holds out her hand to help me up. "Come on, let's have a shower together before we go. It's going to be hard enough to keep my hands off you all day and I think we both need something to keep us going."

30

"I've had a wonderful day," I say as we're sitting in the back of the van that's heading toward the homeless shelter. "The driver was super nice, and his wife and kids were just lovely."

"I know, right? Plus, his wife makes the best waffles." Zelda puts her arm around me and squeezes me. Even now, at ten p.m., she seems full of energy, and I feel the same way. I guess we're both a little hyped up from all the holiday fun.

"Is it weird to say that I'm a little disappointed that it's almost over?" I ask with a chuckle. "I've really enjoyed this. The look on the kid's faces, the excitement, all the wonderful homes we've visited..." I roll my eyes. "Wonderful but weird."

Zelda laughs too. "So true. What about that second home? A life-sized stainless-steel reindeer standing over the dining table? Who does that?"

"Yeah, that was something else." I cup her face and kiss her as the van comes to a halt.

"We're here," the driver says. "I'll help you unload, and someone called Frank will meet you inside."

From the sign above the door, I see this used to be a gymnasium, but it's now filled with rows of cots and there's a makeshift kitchen in the left-hand corner just as we come in. Zelda doesn't bother with her Santa act as there are no children here, and warm clothes and food is the priority, not entertainment. Still, we receive Christmas greetings, cheers and friendly smiles as we walk in, and a couple of dirty Santa jokes are thrown at us for good measure. It amazes me that despite their situation, most of the people staying here are in good spirits.

"Thank you so much for this, guys, you have no idea what this means to us," Frank, a tall, skinny man with long gray hair and an equally long beard says as he shows us around.

"Don't thank us." Zelda smiles at him. "We're just doing the drop-off but it's an honor to do so."

The rectangular gymnasium holds fifty beds of which all are occupied tonight. Behind the stove and a make-shift counter, six volunteers are making hot drinks and spooning stew and dumplings into bowls, serving the line of homeless who may not have eaten all day. It breaks my heart to imagine them having to sleep outside in the snow and although this is far from my life right now, I genuinely believe my mother and I may have been in the same position if she hadn't been lucky enough to find a job so soon after my father left. Half of them are seniors who are too old to work and if it wasn't for organizations like this, they wouldn't survive the winter.

After a chat with Frank who runs the place, we place all the bags against the back wall and people start to gather around us to see what we've brought. There are winter coats, blankets, sweaters, scarves, gloves and dozens of pairs of socks, along with two huge boxes filled with chocolate and cookies.

"What can I do to help?" I ask.

"Oh, you want to help?" Frank seems surprised as he scratches his beard. "Well, if you don't mind, you could take the boxes with candy to the kitchen area and fill some of the trays with a selection." He regards me, then glances at Zelda. "I'm sure you guys are busy but if you're not, we're having some musicians in later for a little sing-along, so you could stay for that if you'd like?"

Zelda looks at me and smiles. "I'm happy to stay if you are?"

"Absolutely. If you need help…"

Frank nods and claps his hands together. "Yes, we could really do with an extra pair of hands, actually. Everyone gets one set of clothing and anything we're not handing out here will be distributed to our other centers across New York, so they need to be put in separate bags per size."

"No problem. Then I'll do that while my little helper takes care of the treats." Zelda shoots me a wink and starts unpacking the boxes.

An hour later, we're sitting on the floor on cushions in a big circle, singing along to a Michael Bublé impersonator who is belting out his latest Christmas album. He's not the best singer, but his enthusiasm makes up for that. Standing in the middle with a speaker next to him, he gets everyone to join in with 'White Christmas'. The mood within the bare walls of the big space has shifted and although the circumstances are sad, it feels oddly festive tonight. The old woman next to me who introduced herself as Maggie, gives me a toothless grin as she puts an arm around my shoulders and sings her heart out.

For a moment, it feels like everyone has forgotten about their troubles and how to get through the next day. Tonight is just about the here and now, and it brings tears to my eyes. It hits me then that I'm fucking lucky. I have a roof over my head, food on my plate, I have my mom and I have good friends. I'm rich in love and support and vow to never complain about my life again.

Zelda is getting sucked in too; she's sitting opposite me in the circle between a man and a woman who are both wearing their new clothes. One is also wearing her Santa beard and the other her red fur-lined hat, and they're holding hands as they sway from side to side, laughing at their attempts to harmonize. I stare at her and my heart swells. If I'm planning on making new memories, this is the best way to start.

31

———

"I never thought I'd say this, but I'm going to miss this costume." Zelda peels off the layers of her Santa suit before tossing them into a clothing bag. "I hope they won't mind that the beard and hat are missing; Sinéad and Andrew were so excited about them that I didn't have the heart to ask for them back."

"You're sweet," I say as I help her remove the thermal pantyhose she was wearing under the suit before taking off my own elf outfit. "And yes, I'm going to miss it too. Maybe I should hire you a suit next year. You know... just for fun." The fact that I'm referring to 'next year' is enormous for me and I'm about to apologize for saying it when I see Zelda's mouth pull into a smile.

"Next year?" she repeats, running a hand through my hair before pulling me in.

"Yeah." I'm not going to take it back; it's how I feel right now. "If we're still together," I add. Thinking about a long-term relationship with someone would have scared the crap out of me only a month ago but since meeting Zelda, my whole outlook on life has changed. Sure, we haven't known each other long, but this feels right and most importantly, I trust her. Our chemistry is rare; I know that, and what I feel for her is like nothing I've ever felt. It's special, spectacular and overwhelming in so many ways that even if this doesn't work out, I know I will feel lucky to have had her in my life. She's teaching me to live in the here and now, and that's exactly where I want to be.

"I don't know what's happened to you overnight, but I like your thinking." Zelda murmurs against my lips.

"You've opened up my mind," I whisper. "Thank you for that."

"Glad I managed to change your perspective." Zelda steps back and fixes her eyes on my naked body. "And as far as the costumes are concerned... We can have fun without them." She smiles. "Or I could order you something online? A maid's costume, or a cheerleader one, perhaps?"

I laugh and feel a blush creep onto my cheeks. From the look on her face, I imagine she's going through a million different scenarios in her head. "What's your ultimate fantasy?"

"I may have to think about that because when it comes to you, there's no end to them." She grins and leans in to kiss my neck. "How about you study your cute little ass off while I start rehearsals and I'll bring something over to your dorm room next week?"

"That sounds like a plan."

"But for now..." Zelda nibbles at my skin and I close my eyes at the delicious sting it causes. "I have something I think you might like." She walks over to the kitchen table and picks up a shiny white bag that's been sitting on one of the chairs. "Merry Christmas."

"Is this for me?" I bite my lip in regret. "But I didn't get you anything and..."

"No need, silly," Zelda interrupts me. "I was just wandering through Bergman's after my shift the other day and found something I thought you might like, with your passion for lingerie and all..." She shrugs and smiles mischievously. "I hope I got the size right. Anyway, it's just as much my present as it's yours because I'm dying to see you in it."

"Hmm..." I open the bag that contains a smaller bag, branded with one of my favorite labels. Inside, wrapped in baby pink silk paper, is a gorgeous white lingerie set. The outfit, which comprises of a lace bodice with matching garter belt, a pair of skin-colored thigh high stockings with lace edges, and a knee-length cover-up with batwing sleeves made out of the same material make my breath hitch in excitement. Running my hands over the fragile fabric, I can already imagine how it will feel against my skin when I'm wearing it. "It's beautiful."

"Do you like it? I can take it back if you don't..."

"Are you kidding me? I love it. How did you know my size?"

"I checked the labels on your lingerie the other night and took a guess." Zelda looks over the moon with my reaction. "The color is all me though. I've never been drawn to white, but I saw it and thought it would look great on you."

Since I'm already naked, I feel an urge to try it on, so I step into the bodice and the garter belt, then carefully pull up the stockings and secure them. The cover-up falls over my curves like a waterfall and I walk over to the standing mirror by her bed to admire the fine lace. My breasts are barely covered in the low-cut bodice; the plunging neckline showing a lot of cleavage as it almost reaches my navel, but it still gives off an air of elegance and grace.

"God, that's hot." Zelda comes up behind me and rests her chin on my shoulder.

"Thank you," I say again in a soft voice, wondering how she could possibly know me so well already.

"You're welcome." Zelda runs her hand over my exposed cleavage and down to my belly, resting her index finger where the neckline ends in a low 'V'. "I have no idea why this is so fucking sexy. You were just naked and now you're more or less covered up again, so it makes no sense." She chuckles and shrugs. "Although I love the idea of undressing you; I could do that over and over."

"Sometimes it's nice to leave something to the imagination," I whisper, tilting my head to the side to press my cheek against hers.

"That's true." She meets my eyes in our reflection and her face tells me her thoughts are far from pure. "There's something very virginal about the white..."

"Virginal, huh?" I turn around and brazenly push my body against hers. "Perhaps you'd like to fantasize about that as you unwrap your present?"

EPILOGUE

"I can't believe I'm sitting in the front row at a Broadway show." My mother couldn't be happier. She's dolled up to the nines, holding hands with Johnny, who's in the seat next to her. "Zelda is going to be so amazing. Was she nervous today?"

"Yeah, of course she was," I say. "It's her first night, but she's going to do great."

"Nerves are healthy," Johnny agrees. "She'd be fooling herself if she said she wasn't." He leans over my mother to pat my shoulder. "And you're right; she'll be great. That woman has a presence about her."

My mother's new 'friend' as she calls him, is looking dapper too, dressed in a navy suit, white shirt and an electric blue tie. His gray afro is held back by a navy hairband and I've noticed he's even matched his socks for the occasion. This is the man responsible for my mother acting like a teenager for the past couple of months and I couldn't be happier for them. Johnny's a great cook and Zelda and I have been over for dinner at his house, where he cooked up a Caribbean feast.

Seeing my mother so chilled and in love has changed my life for the better too. Knowing Johnny's looking after her, I don't worry about her as much anymore, and I've become more relaxed myself, taking every day as it comes instead of always planning ahead.

Tonight, I'm wearing my new black satin off the shoulder dress and I have no doubt Zelda is going to love my outfit as well as what's underneath it. I can't think of a better way to celebrate her first night than surprising her with the hot red lingerie set I'm wearing.

The show hasn't even started and I'm already bursting with pride. She's worked hard, getting up early to go to the gym in the mornings and rehearsing until late at night, especially in the past two weeks. Her long days have allowed me to study in peace, though, as I've spent most of my days and nights holed up in her studio.

The best part of the day is waking up early together and having an hour in bed before she leaves. When my internship starts next month, well, I guess we'll have to set our alarms even earlier. We'll both be super busy and on entirely different schedules but that's not something I worry about.

Life with Zelda is easy and at the same time overwhelmingly exciting. Together we've embarked on a sexual journey of daring, giving, taking, receiving, asking and exploring, and I love purposely breaking her rules and getting punished for it.

The cheerleader and maid costumes arrived along with a whole bunch of other stuff Zelda ordered, and we've had a lot of fun with them. Other nights, we make love like it's our last night on earth, with a pureness that's both tender and passionate. She's my rock and I'm hers, and although we couldn't be more different, our relationship works with an effortless flow.

When the lights in the theatre are dimmed and the curtains open, butterflies take over and I squeeze my mother's hand. The audience falls silent, and instantly there's a buzz of excitement and anticipation in the air.

The announcer's heavy voice blasts through the theatre: "Welcome. Ladies and Gentlemen, you are about to see a story of murder, greed, corruption, violence, exploitation, adultery, and treachery. Enjoy the show."

Holding my breath and subconsciously tapping my heeled foot to the beat of the song I've heard so many times while she rehearsed at home, my heart races when the spotlight comes on. Blending in with the ensemble of similarly dressed actors, I almost don't recognize Zelda at first, dressed in a black crop top and hotpants, and sporting a black Velma Kelly wig. But when she steps away from the group to the front of the stage and sings her first line there's no mistake. There she is. The woman I love. My girl.

AFTERWORD

I hope you've loved reading *Santa's Favorite* as much as I've loved writing it. If you've enjoyed this book, would you consider rating it and reviewing it on www.amazon.com? Reviews are very important to authors and I'd be really grateful.

ALSO BY MADELEINE TAYLOR

The Good Girl

Online

Masquerade